# A triple-header of Dan Gutman's Baseball Card Adventures!

## Praise for HONUS & ME:

"An enjoyable escape into another decade."
—*School Library Journal*

"This novel hits at least a triple!"
—*Publishers Weekly*

## Praise for JACKIE & ME:

"Fans of America's favorite pastime will particularly appreciate the details and some of the descriptions of some great games, including the 1947 World Series."
—*School Library Journal*

"Dan Gutman has devised a wonderful mechanism for teaching social history while telling a great tale."
—*The Philadelphia Inquirer*

## Praise for BABE & ME:

"Readers will enjoy the action, the rich baseball lore, and the sense of adventure."
—ALA *Booklist*

"The book convincingly captures Babe's oversized personality."
—*The Horn Book*

# SHOELESS JOE *& Me*

*A Baseball Card Adventure*

# Dan Gutman

SCHOLASTIC INC.

New York  Toronto  London  Auckland  Sydney
Mexico City  New Delhi  Hong Kong  Buenos Aires

ISBN 0-439-65357-6

Copyright © 2002 by Dan Gutman. All rights reserved.
Published by Scholastic Inc., 557 Broadway, New York, NY 10012,
by arrangement with HarperCollins Publishers. SCHOLASTIC and associated logos
are trademarks and/or registered trademarks of Scholastic Inc.

24 23 22 21 20 19 18 17 16 15 14          6 7 8 9/0

Printed in the U.S.A.          40

First Scholastic printing, April 2004

**Dedicated to the great kids,
teachers, and librarians at the
schools I visited in 2000**

# Acknowledgments

Special thanks to the following people for all their help: Bill Francis and Bill Burdick at the National Baseball Hall of Fame; Mark Alvarez and David Pietrusza of The Society for American Baseball Research; Jake Hamlin and Lester Erwin of The Shoeless Joe Jackson Society; Cynthia Keller of the Cincinnati Museum Center; Dr. Jonathan Cohen and Dr. Scott Kolander; Gina Kolata; Mary Brace; Allen Barra; and my wife, Nina Wallace, for her wonderful artwork.

Many thanks also to the great people I met at the schools I visited in 2000:

In New Jersey: Union Street School in Margate, Moorestown Middle School in Moorestown, Crescent School in Waldwick, Harrington Park School in Harrington Park, Churchill School in Fairfield, Bellmawr Park School in Bellmawr, Costello School in Brooklawn, Neeta School in Medford Lakes, Allen School

# ACKNOWLEDGMENTS

in Medford, Simmons School in Clayton, Lore School in Ewing, Somerville School in Ridgewood, Central Middle School in Parsippany, Rockaway Valley School in Boonton Township, Durand School in Vineland, Bedminster School in Bedminster, Warnsdorfer School in East Brunswick, Central School in Warren, Green-Fields School in West Deptford, Logan School in Swedesboro, Tatem School in Haddonfield, Central School in East Brunswick, Wantage School in Sussex, North Boulevard School in Pompton Plains, Haviland Avenue School in Audubon, Gregory School in West Orange, Avalon School in Avalon, and Yavneh Academy in Paramus.

In Texas: Willow Creek, Lakewood, Tomball Elementary, and Tomball Intermediate in Tomball; Felix Tijerina School in Houston; Stephens School in Aldine; Ride, Bush, Powell, Galatas, Hailey, and Collins schools in The Woodlands; Forman and Wells schools in Plano; Miller School in Richardson; Pinkerton, Mockingbird, Cottonwood, North Middle, Denton Creek, Lakeside, Austin, St. John's, Lee, Valley Ranch, Wilson, West Middle, Town Center, and East Middle schools in Coppell; Greenhill School in Addison; and West Memorial, Hutsell, Nottingham, Pattison, Mayde Creek, Winborn, and Wolfe schools in Katy.

In Oklahoma: Bishop John Carroll, Oakdale, Wiley Post, Rollingwood, Downs, Will Rogers, Harvest Hills, Dennis, Kirkland, Tulakes, Hefner, Cooper, Overholser, Central Intermediate, and Western Oaks Middle School in Oklahoma City; Sequoyah and Cimarron middle schools in Edmond; Jenks East School in Jenks; and Darnaby School in Tulsa.

# ACKNOWLEDGMENTS

In Pennsylvania: Selinsgrove Intermediate in Selinsgrove; Calypso, Clearview, and Fountain Hill schools in Bethlehem; New Cumberland School in New Cumberland; Allen and Camp Hill schools in Camp Hill; Crossroads School in Lewisberry; Lemoyne School in Lemoyne; Eagle View and Good Hope schools in Mechanicsburg; Big Spring School in Newville; Wilson School in Carlisle; East Pennsboro School in Enola; Garwood Middle School in Fairview; and Erie Day School in Erie.

In New York: Chapel and Bronxville schools in Bronxville; Lakeview School in Mahopac; Meadow Pond School in South Salem; Lewisboro School in Lewisboro; and Baker, Kennedy, and Lakeville schools in Great Neck.

In Connecticut: Hopewell and Buttonball schools in South Glastonbury; West, East, and South schools in New Canaan; and Ox Ridge and Holmes schools in Darien.

In Iowa: Twain and Jefferson schools in Bettendorf; St. Paul's School in Davenport; and Mulberry, West, Colorado, Grant, McKinley, Washington, Jefferson, Franklin, Madison, Hayes, and Central middle schools in Muscatine.

In South Carolina: East End, Greenwood High, Merrywood, Mathews, Oakland, Pinecrest, Hodges, Lakeview, and Ware Shoals schools in Greenwood.

In Illinois: Crone and Gregory middle schools in Naperville and Granger Middle School in Aurora.

In Florida: Shorecrest School in St. Petersburg and St. Mary's and Berkeley schools in Tampa.

In Delaware: North Georgetown School in Georgetown and East Millsboro School in Millsboro.

# The 1919 Chicago White Sox

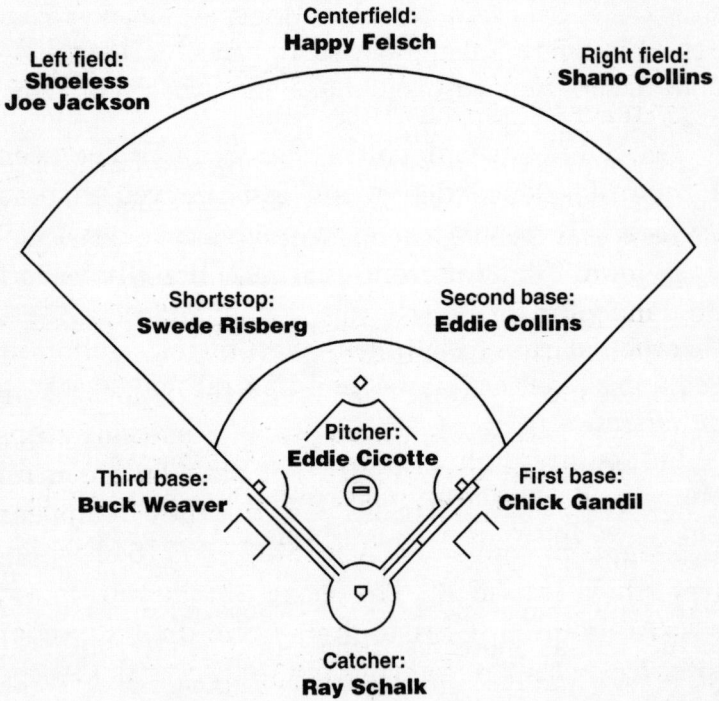

Centerfield:
**Happy Felsch**

Left field:
**Shoeless
Joe Jackson**

Right field:
**Shano Collins**

Shortstop:
**Swede Risberg**

Second base:
**Eddie Collins**

Pitcher:
**Eddie Cicotte**

Third base:
**Buck Weaver**

First base:
**Chick Gandil**

Catcher:
**Ray Schalk**

# The Power

I CAN TRAVEL THROUGH TIME.

Oh, I know what you're thinking. You've seen dozens of science fiction movies and you've read books where people travel through time. But I can really *do* it. The difference is that I don't have any time machine.

I do it with baseball cards.

In the movies, time machines usually look like a booth, sort of like a bathroom stall. Somebody steps inside, and they turn a bunch of dials on a control panel. They push a button, and *zap*, they disappear and reappear conveniently in 1492 or 1776 or whenever they intended. The next thing you know, they're helping Christopher Columbus discover America or they're fighting the British with George Washington.

Well, it doesn't work that way. At least not for

me. I don't have a time machine or some fancy car like that kid had in *Back to the Future*. My baseball cards serve as my ticket to another time. And they don't always work the way I want them to.

You don't have to believe me. I don't expect you to. But one day I happened to be holding a valuable 1909 Honus Wagner baseball card, and I began to feel a strange tingling sensation in my fingertips. It was like I had slept on my arm all night or something. But it was more of a pleasant, buzzy feeling.

The tingling moved up my arm and washed over my body. About five seconds later, I was in the year 1909. I swear to you, it *happened*. I actually got to meet Honus Wagner, the Hall of Fame shortstop of the Pittsburgh Pirates. It was the most amazing thing that ever happened to me.

Finding myself in 1909 was exciting and more than a little frightening. I almost didn't make it back home. Luckily, I happened to be carrying a few new baseball cards at the time. I used one of them to send myself back to the present day.

Since that experience, I've taken other journeys through time. I got a 1947 Jackie Robinson card and watched him become the first African American in sixty years to play in the major leagues. I got a 1932 Babe Ruth card and watched him hit the most famous and controversial home run in baseball history.

I thought I was getting pretty good at traveling through time with baseball cards. But none of those trips prepared me for what happened when I went on a journey to the year 1919. That's what this story is about.

Joe Stoshack

# 1

## No Fair

"I'LL GIVE YOU FIVE BUCKS IF YOU GET A HIT RIGHT NOW, Stoshack," our shortstop Greg Horwitz yelled to me. "I'm late for my soccer game."

I wiped my nose on my sleeve and knocked the dirt off my cleats. Yeah, I was going to get a hit. I could feel it in my bones. And we needed one pretty badly.

The guys on my team didn't call it "Little League" anymore. We were all thirteen now, and we were in the majors. That doesn't mean major-league quality or anything like that, but we could play the game.

In our league, you didn't see kids getting bonked on the head by easy pop-ups like you did when we were in the minors. You didn't see kids crying when they struck out. You didn't see kids standing around the outfield watching planes fly by. We came to play ball. By this time, the kids who couldn't hack it had switched to playing musical instruments or doing art or whatever kids do who don't play sports anymore.

I live in Louisville, Kentucky, which in case you don't know is just across the Ohio River from Indiana. The Kentucky Derby—a famous horse race—is held here each May. But since I'm a baseball fan, my favorite part of town is the Louisville Slugger Museum on West Main Street. They've got a baseball bat outside that's six stories high.

I wiped my nose again and looked over at Coach Tropiano standing in foul territory near third base. He clapped his hands together twice, then rubbed the palm of his right hand across the words "Flip's Fan Club" on his shirt. The swing away sign. Good. No way I want to be bunting at a time like this.

I wiped away some more snot and wished my nose would stop running. I was just getting over the flu, but I hadn't quite shaken it yet. My mom didn't want me to play until I was all better. But it was the play-offs! If I waited until I was all better, the season would be over.

"Five bucks, Stoshack," Horwitz hollered as I walked up to the plate.

"Give ya ten if ya strike out," the catcher cracked.

"And I will eject both of you young men from the game if you continue this line of discussion," warned the umpire, Mr. Kane, the science teacher at my school who umpires some of our games in his spare time. The catcher and I looked at him, and then at each other. What a spoilsport! The guy has no sense of humor.

I got into the batter's box and dug my right cleat into the dirt five inches from the plate.

"C'mon, Joey," my mom shouted from the third-base bleachers. "Blast one outta here, baby!"

It had taken a long time, but I had finally taught my mom enough baseball chatter so she wouldn't make a fool of herself. Used to be, she would shout the lamest things when I came to bat. Stuff like, "Hit a touchdown!" Sometimes I would have to pretend I wasn't related to her.

I wiped more snot off my nose and glanced at the scoreboard. 5-5. The bases were loaded. One out. Bottom of the sixth. Last inning of a one-game play-off between us and Yampell Jewelers. Nothing like a little pressure to get a guy motivated.

If I could drive in Chase, our runner on third, we'd win the Louisville Little League Championship. If I couldn't, the game would end in a tie and we'd have to play Yampell again next Saturday. The Little League officials are convinced that our thirteen-year-old bodies are too frail and fragile to play extra innings. Me, I could play all day.

The pitcher stared at me. I pumped my bat across the plate a few times to show him I meant business. Mentally, I counted the seven things that could happen that would get that winning run home.

*1. I could get a hit and be the hero, of course. That would be my preference.*

*2. I could draw a walk and force the run in.*

*3. Somebody could make an error.*

*4. The pitcher could throw a wild pitch.*

*5. There could be a passed ball.*

*6. I could fly out to the outfield, and Chase could tag up and score.*

*7. I could ground out, and the runner on third would score on the play.*

The pitcher looked nervous. I licked my lips.

"Let's go, Matthew!" somebody yelled from the first-base bleachers. "Strike this guy out."

"If you ever get a hit in your whole life," Chase yelled through cupped hands, "get one *now!*"

I blinked my eyes hard a few times in the hope that I wouldn't have to blink when the ball was coming toward the plate.

I really didn't want to have to play these guys again next Saturday. Half the guys on our team would be away at a soccer tournament in Lexington. They happened to be our best players. The soccer coach hates baseball and gets crazy if any of his players miss a soccer game to play baseball. But baseball is the only game I play. I really wanted to end the game *now*.

The pitcher went into his windup and reared back to throw. When the ball was about halfway to the plate, I suddenly realized there was another thing that could happen that would bring the runner on third home.

*8. I could get hit by a pitch.*

The ball was coming straight at my head.

I don't know if you've ever been in a situation like this, but there's no way to think rationally. You just let your instincts tell you what to do, like a wild animal trying to survive in the jungle.

I bailed out of the batter's box, my bat flying one way and my helmet flying another way. The ball whizzed past my nose as I flopped in the dirt. When I looked up, the catcher had the ball in his glove.

"Did it hit me?" I asked Mr. Kane hopefully.

"No such luck, Mr. Stoshack," he replied. "Ball one."

When it was clear that I wasn't hurt, my teammates started razzing me.

"Oh man, Stoshack! Why didn't you let it hit you?"

"Yeah, how about taking one for the team, Stosh?"

"Shut up, Miller." I got up and spanked the dirt off my pants. My biggest fear was that my mother might run out of the stands to see if I was okay. She stayed put, knowing full well that if she put one foot on the field, I would be so humiliated that I would refuse to speak to her for a week.

I took my time collecting my bat and helmet. My heart was beating fast. I forgot all about my runny nose. *If the next pitch is close*, I thought to myself, *I'll let it nick me.*

Mr. Kane walked halfway to the mound. "In light of the situation," he informed the pitcher, "I will assume you were not trying to hit Mr. Stoshack with that pitch. Is that correct?"

"It got away from me," the pitcher explained.

"See that it doesn't happen again, young man," Mr. Kane warned. "We have not had a fatality all season, and I do not want one now."

"What's a fatality?" the pitcher asked.

"Look it up when you get home," Mr. Kane grumbled as he walked back to brush off the plate.

"Throw another pitch like that," the catcher shouted, "and I'll kill you. *Then* you'll know what it means."

The pitcher fidgeted and looked in for the sign. I got set in the batter's box.

The pitch came in, but this time it was so far outside that the catcher had to dive for it. He made a spectacular stop. Chase came halfway down the third baseline, then scampered back to the bag.

"Ball two!" called Mr. Kane.

"Nice stop," I muttered to the catcher.

"Hit the mitt, will you?" he barked to his pitcher as he returned the ball. "What is your problem?"

"It got away from me," the pitcher explained.

"See that it don't happen again," the catcher barked.

"*Doesn't*," corrected Mr. Kane. "See that it *doesn't* happen again."

"Get it over, Matthew!" somebody yelled from the bleachers.

I got ready again. 2-0 count. Big advantage to me. He *had* to throw a strike on the next pitch or the count would be 3-0 and he would *really* be in danger of walking in the winning run.

"Your pitch, Stosh!" Chase yelled from third.

It *was* my pitch. Right down the middle of the plate, about belt high. Juicy as a Fuddruckers burger. I attacked it, just like the coach told us to. The faster the bat moves, the harder it hits the ball.

I made solid contact, smashing the ball up the middle. It took a hop about halfway to the pitcher. He ducked, throwing his glove in front of his face in self-defense. As I dug for first, I saw the ball hit his glove and roll down the back of the pitcher's mound.

"Second base!" screamed the catcher.

The pitcher pounced on the ball and flipped it underhand to the second baseman.

At that point, I didn't see the rest of the play. I was digging for first with everything I had. If they made the force play at second, that would be two outs. Then the second baseman would throw to first and try to make a game-ending double play. If I could beat the throw, Chase would score from third and we would win. I pushed myself to run faster than I had ever run before.

As I streaked toward the bag, I saw the first

baseman stretching and reaching with his glove. It was going to be close. I strained to get my foot on the bag before the ball reached him. A split second after my foot hit first base, I heard the pop of the ball smacking into the first baseman's glove. I was safe.

"You're out!" Mr. Kane shouted.

"What!" I turned around and charged toward him.

"I was safe!" I screamed. "I beat it!"

"Mr. Stoshack," he replied calmly, "I would eject you from the game for that remark, but unfortunately the game is over. The final score is 5-5. Next Saturday, you had better show some respect and sportsmanship or you will be ejected in the first inning."

"I was safe," I insisted. "What are you, blind? Oh, man, we would've won the game! That's not fair!"

# 2

# Bad News

I MIGHT HAVE GONE COMPLETELY OUT OF CONTROL when the umpire called me out, but a strong arm wrapped around my shoulder and steered me away from the infield. I could tell without looking that it was the strong arm of Flip Valentini.

"Fuhgetuhboutit, Stosh."

Flip grew up in Brooklyn, where "fuhgetuhboutit" apparently is how they say "forget about it." He's the owner of Flip's Fan Club, a little sports card shop in downtown Louisville that sponsors our team. He's an old gray-haired guy but cooler than most grown-ups I've met.

"I *won't* forget about it!" I complained. "It's not fair! I was safe! If the ump hadn't blown the call, we would have won the championship."

"It's over," Flip said. "Nothin' you can do. So he blew the call. In the long run, it all evens out."

Flip walked me around the outfield while I

cooled down. Usually you never meet the people who sponsor your teams. But Flip comes out to all our games and even to some of our practices. He's sort of like a dad to some of the kids on the team like me, whose parents are divorced. Flip usually brings along packs of baseball cards to pass out to the kids on the team, but the last few games he didn't bring any.

At our first practice back in March, Flip told us that all his life he wanted to own his own baseball team. It costs something like a million dollars to buy even a minor league team, and he didn't have anywhere near that kind of money. So he invested five hundred dollars to sponsor our team. It must give him a special thrill to see the words "Flip's Fan Club" on the front of our uniforms.

"It's just not fair," I continued to whine. "I was safe."

"You *were* safe, Stosh." Flip sighed. "And it's *not* fair. But life isn't always fair. You're gonna realize that someday."

That's when Flip started telling me the story of Shoeless Joe Jackson.

"He was one of the great ones," Flip told me as we walked the grass in left field. "He batted .356 from 1908 to 1920. That's the third-highest average of all time. He hit over .370 in four seasons. He was maybe the greatest natural hitter who ever lived. Babe Ruth even said he patterned his swing after Shoeless Joe's."

"No kidding?"

"No kiddin', Stosh. Jackson had this dark bat. Black Betsy, he called it. It was like his baby. He took it with him everywhere. They say he used to sleep with it. He was a great outfielder, too. Ty Cobb said Joe was the best he ever saw."

"So how come I never heard of him?" I asked. "Why isn't he in the Baseball Hall of Fame?"

"Because life isn't always fair, Stosh."

Flip told me the story of the Black Sox Scandal. The 1919 Chicago White Sox were one of the greatest teams ever. They cruised to the American League pennant. They were heavy favorites to win the World Series against the Cincinnati Reds. But they played poorly and lost. Later, it came out that eight members of the White Sox had lost the World Series on purpose.

"Why'd they do that?"

"They were paid off by gamblers to lose," Flip explained, "and they got caught. People called 'em the Black Sox, and all eight of 'em—including Shoeless Joe Jackson—were banned from baseball for the rest of their lives. That's after they were declared innocent when they were put on trial."

"That's not fair."

"No, it wasn't. Like I said, Stosh, life isn't always fair. The Black Sox Scandal is one of the saddest stories in the history of sport."

I was still upset about the blown call at first base, but I no longer wanted to do physical harm to Mr. Kane. Flip walked me back to our bench, where the other kids were packing their bats and gloves and stuff.

"Listen up!" Flip hollered. "I have an announcement to make."

I found a spot on the bench next to Chase Hathaway.

"Boys, I wanted to tell you something before rumors start spreading around school," Flip announced. "Flip's Fan Club is closing."

"What?" we all yelled.

"My rent was doubled," Flip explained. "I can't afford to keep the store open anymore."

"That's not fair!" a few of us complained, and Flip shot me a look.

"What about the team?" Chase asked.

"Don't worry. Next season there will be a different sponsor."

"What are you gonna do, Flip?" I asked.

"Retire," Flip replied. "Finally I'll have the time to do all the things I couldn't do the last sixty years. But I wanted to let you guys know the store will be open for another week, so stop in because everything will be on sale. I gotta clean the place out."

Flip walked to the parking lot slowly. I didn't believe for a minute that he was looking forward to retirement. He seemed to enjoy the store so much. We all sat on the bench for a minute, stunned.

"So *that's* why he hasn't been giving out any baseball cards lately," Chase said. "He can't afford to."

"Man, we should hold a fund-raiser or something,"

Greg Horwitz suggested. "I bet if we did a car wash we could make a lot of money. Maybe we could save Flip's store."

"Forget it," our centerfielder, Max Harley, said. "My mom's beauty shop is on the same block as Flip's. Her rent is over a thousand bucks—each month!"

Everybody whistled. I had no idea it cost so much to run a store. You'd have to sell a lot of baseball cards to make a thousand bucks.

"So what can we do?" I asked.

"Nothin'," Chase said. He slung his bat bag over his shoulder, kicked up the kickstand on his bike, and rode off toward home.

# 3

# An Idea

MY MOM USED TO DRIVE ME HOME FROM MY GAMES when I was in the minors, but once I reached the majors most of the other guys walked home, rollerbladed, or rode their bikes. They started to kid me about riding home with "mommy," so I gently told her that I wanted to ride my bike home. She was a little hurt by it, but she said she remembered what it was like trying not to be uncool as a kid.

As I pedaled home from the field, I started thinking about Shoeless Joe Jackson and some of the things Flip had told me. There were a lot of questions going through my mind.

Mom was already in the kitchen preparing dinner when I got home.

"You were safe, honey," she said, "by a mile."

"I know."

"How are you feeling?" she asked as I threw my

bat bag in the closet. "I saw you wiping your nose quite a bit out there."

"I'm getting better."

Mom's a nurse, and she finds sickness and health a lot more interesting than I do.

"Did you take your medicine this morning?"

"Yeah. Hey, Mom, is gambling wrong?"

"Have you been talking with your father?" she asked, a stern look crossing her face. One of the reasons my parents split up a few years ago was because my dad spent a lot of money betting on horse races, football pools, card games, and things like that. He usually lost. He lives in Louisville, too, but he has his own apartment.

"No," I explained. "Flip Valentini told me about some players on the White Sox a long time ago who got paid off by gamblers to lose the World Series. They got thrown out of baseball for the rest of their lives."

"Oh, yeah," Mom said, filling a pot with water. "I remember seeing some movie about that. *Eight Men Out* or something like that."

"Why would anybody lose on purpose, Mom?"

"I don't know that much about baseball," my mother explained, "but I know that professional athletes didn't always earn millions of dollars the way they do today. Years ago, they were hardly paid any money at all. The gamblers probably offered those players a little money and they couldn't resist. Then the gamblers made fortunes betting on them

to lose. It's a shame. I buy lottery tick[...]
in a while. But gambling is like cigarett[...]
and drugs. It can be addictive. Some peop[...]
your father—start doing it and they can't stop[...]

Every Saturday night Mom and I have "movie night," when we rent a movie and make popcorn. I suggested *Eight Men Out*, and they had a copy of it at our local video store.

As we watched the movie, I realized that those players on the White Sox were taken advantage of by a group of sleazy gamblers. Some of the players didn't even get paid a *penny* for throwing the World Series. And the worst part of all was that Shoeless Joe Jackson—this simple country boy who didn't know any better—would be in the Hall of Fame today if he had simply refused an envelope stuffed with money that somebody left in his hotel room. The movie didn't have a happy ending.

As I was rewinding the tape, an idea started to form in my head. I didn't tell Mom at first, because I wasn't sure if she would go for it. But I couldn't get it out of my mind.

I had successfully used baseball cards to travel back to 1909, 1947, and 1932 to meet Honus Wagner, Jackie Robinson, and Babe Ruth. If I could get a 1919 baseball card, I could go back to that year. And if I could go back to 1919, maybe I could prevent the Black Sox Scandal from ever taking place . . . and help Shoeless Joe Jackson!

# 4

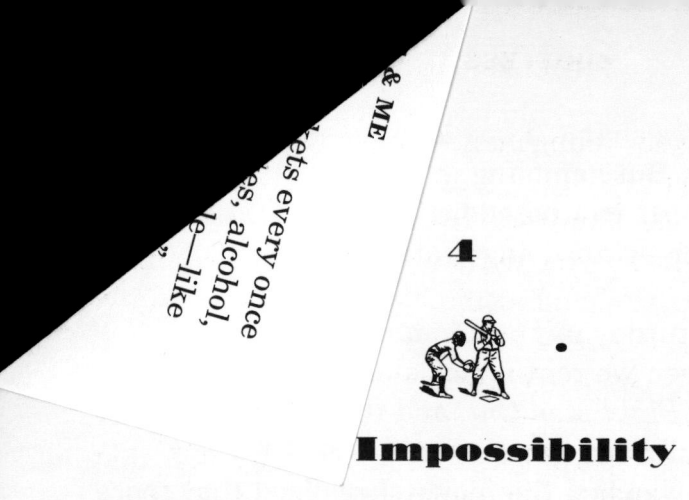

## Impossibility

AS SOON AS MR. KANE SAW ME WALK INTO HIS SCIENCE lab before school on Monday morning, his lips curled up into a smirk. He had been pouring some chemicals into test tubes and getting ready for first period when I came in.

"I suppose you have come to apologize for your unsportsmanlike behavior on Saturday," he said.

Actually, I hadn't come to apologize at all. If anybody should be apologizing, it was Mr. Kane. After all, *he* was the one who blew the call on the play that would have given us the championship. I could have made an issue of it, but I'm no fool.

"I'm sorry," I said as humbly as possible. "I got carried away."

"Apology accepted," Mr. Kane replied. "Such is the folly of youth."

"Mr. Kane, can I ask you a science question?"

"Fire away, young man. Curiosity is the stepping-stone to genius."

"If somebody were to travel back in time—"

Mr. Kane snorted derisively before I could finish and waved his hand at me like a traffic cop telling me to hit the brakes.

"Nobody can travel through time!" he said, raising his voice almost in anger. "The laws of physics simply do not permit it. It is idiocy. Why is it that your generation is so fascinated by the idea of time travel? Maybe you're simply not happy in your own time and think you can escape your problems by living in the future or the past. Is that it, hmm?"

"I know time travel is impossible," I lied. "I'm just curious."

I said Mr. Kane's favorite word on purpose.

"Curious about what?" he asked, a little more gently.

"Well, if somebody *could* travel back in time, would they be able to change history?"

Mr. Kane sighed and shook his head sadly, as if he'd had this discussion before and was sick and tired of it.

"Okay, Joe, let's ignore the fact that time travel is out of the question. Even if it *were* possible, it would still be impossible to change history."

"Why?"

"Take the assassination of Abraham Lincoln as an example," Mr. Kane said. "We all know it happened that terrible evening in 1865. It was in all the newspapers of the time. It is in all our history books. It is in our collective memory. These books and newspapers and memories exist *today*. Nothing can change that. If someone were able to travel back to that night in 1865, they could *not* push the gun away and prevent the bullet from entering Lincoln's head and killing him. If they could, all those books and newspapers and memories would not exist today, don't you see?"

"But if somebody *could* travel back in time and push the gun away," I suggested, "wouldn't the newspapers of 1865 have simply printed that there was an attempt on President Lincoln's life? Wouldn't the time traveler return to the present day to find there were all *new* history books with no mention of Lincoln being assassinated back in 1865?"

"No!"

"Why not?"

"Because it defies logic!" Mr. Kane thundered. "What if somebody went back in time and killed his own great-grandmother before she had children? Would the time traveler then return to the present and find out that he himself did not exist, because his mother had never been born?"

I had no answer for that. But I did know one thing—*I can travel through time.* I can use a baseball card as my time machine. And I could see no reason why I couldn't go back to 1919 and warn Shoeless Joe Jackson that if he accepted money to throw the World Series, he would regret it for the rest of his life.

Now all I had to do was get my hands on a Shoeless Joe Jackson baseball card.

"You're giving me a headache, Mr. Stoshack," Mr. Kane said wearily. "Will you please go to your first period class now?"

# 5

# Have a Nice Trip

THERE WAS A LITTLE TIME LEFT OVER AT THE END OF computer class, so I asked the computer teacher, Mrs. Ducharme, if I could log on to eBay, the on-line auction site. She gave me the okay, as long as I didn't buy or sell anything on school time.

I typed in www.ebay.com and did a search for "Shoeless Joe." A long list of items popped up. Shoeless Joe photos. Shoeless Joe books. Shoeless Joe this. Shoeless Joe that. Somebody was even selling an old sign showing Shoeless Joe endorsing *shoes*! But nobody was selling a Shoeless Joe Jackson baseball card.

"Did you find what you wanted?" Mrs. Ducharme asked me when the bell rang.

"No, but I'll keep looking."

When school was over, I rode my bike over to Flip's Fan Club, which is about a mile from school.

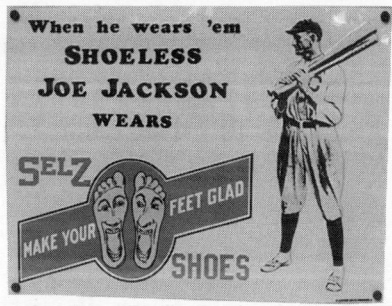

**Somebody was even selling an old sign showing
Shoeless Joe Jackson endorsing shoes!**

There was a hand-lettered sign in the window:
RETIREMENT SALE! 10% OFF EVERYTHING INSIDE.

Flip's is probably my favorite store in the world.
I don't have a zillion baseball cards or anything, but
I like to go there anyway. It's a tiny little hole in the
wall, just big enough for Flip's chair, a long glass
display case, and four walls jam-packed with sports
cards and cool collectibles. Kids are always hanging around, swapping cards, making deals, talking
sports.

On Friday nights, Flip keeps the store open late
so kids can come in and flip cards. It's a game that
Flip says he used to play when he was a kid grow-
ing up in Brooklyn. In fact, that's how he got the
nickname "Flip."

Here's how you play. Two kids each toss a card
against the wall. Whoever's card lands closest to the
wall gets to keep both cards. Flip doesn't even make

any money from it. He just does it so kids in town have a safe place to go on Friday night. Of course, Friday Night at Flip's would be coming to an end when the store closes for good.

Flip was behind the counter reading the newspaper when I came in. The walls were not completely covered by merchandise, as they usually were. I guess Flip was starting to sell off his inventory in preparation for shutting down the shop. For a change, there weren't any kids hanging around.

"Stosh!" he said cheerfully, looking up from his paper.

"I'm glad the store is still open."

"I gotta clear my stuff outta here a week from today."

"What are you gonna do after that?"

"Putter around, I s'pose."

"It's not fair that they doubled your rent, Flip."

"Again with the not fair." He chuckled. "Remember what I told you on Saturday?"

"Life isn't always fair," I recalled. "And you told me about Shoeless Joe Jackson."

"That's right," Flip said. "Whenever I think somethin' isn't fair, I think about what happened to Shoeless Joe. It makes me appreciate that whatever happened to me wasn't so terrible after all."

"I want to ask you a question about Shoeless Joe," I said. "If he accepted money from gamblers to lose the World Series, didn't he *deserve* to be thrown out of baseball? I mean, he did a really bad thing, didn't he? Didn't he deserve to be punished?"

"There's one thing I didn't tell you about Shoeless Joe," Flip said. "He was illiterate."

"You mean he didn't know how to read?"

"Or write," Flip explained, turning around to pull out a thick book from the shelf behind him. "It wasn't any secret. A lot of people were illiterate back then. Shoeless Joe Jackson never went to school. By the time he was your age, Stosh, he was already working twelve hours a day in a cotton mill in South Carolina."

The book Flip pulled off the shelf was titled *Famous Autographs*. Flip flipped through the pages until he got to the letter *J*.

"Look at this," he said, pointing his stubby finger at the page when he found the name "*Jackson*." There were a bunch of autographs of famous Jacksons—Stonewall, Reggie, Michael, Andrew, Jesse. But one of them stood out from all the rest— Joseph Jefferson ("Shoeless Joe") Jackson. The signature looked like it had been written by a first grader.

BEST REGARDS
JOE JACKSON

Flip pulled out a magnifying glass and held it over the signature.

"Notice the block letters," Flip pointed out. "All caps. Look at the way he made the letter *A*. See the loop in the *J*?"

"How could he write the words 'best regards' if he was illiterate?"

"Shoeless Joe was embarrassed that he couldn't read or write. He used to carry around a scrap of paper in his pocket wherever he went. The paper said, 'Best Regards, Joe Jackson' on it. His wife had written it out for him. When somebody asked him for an autograph, he would pull out the paper and carefully copy the letters. It would take him about fifteen minutes to write 'best regards.' Usually he would just have his wife sign autographs for him. That's why almost all the Shoeless Joe Jackson autographs floating around among collectors are actually his wife's autograph."

"So his autograph must be really valuable, huh?"

"More than valuable, Stosh." Flip smiled. "It's the *most* valuable autograph of the last two hundred years. There are only *three known samples* of Shoeless Joe's writing that exist. The last time one was sold, the seller got five hundred thousand dollars for it."

"A half a million bucks!" I said, letting out a whistle. Flip closed the book and put it back on the shelf.

"See, the poor guy was a genius at playin' ball," Flip explained, "but he was a dummy at everything else. He didn't know what he was doin' when he took that money from those gamblers. He didn't throw the World Series. He had the best Series of anybody on the field. Poor Shoeless Joe got thrown out of baseball and died in disgrace. He didn't have a dime to his name."

I had been waiting for the right moment to pop my question to Flip. It seemed like the right time.

"Do you have a Shoeless Joe Jackson baseball card from 1919?" I asked.

"Nah," he replied. "They go for somethin' like twenty-three thousand dollars."

My heart sank.

"Whaddaya want a Shoeless Joe card for?" Flip asked.

"I can't tell you."

"Why not?"

"You wouldn't believe me."

"Try me."

"You'll just laugh."

"I won't. I promise."

Up until now, only my mom and dad knew about the power I had with baseball cards. I hadn't told anybody at school or anyone on my baseball team. I figured they would think I was crazy or something.

"Okay." I sighed, looking Flip in the eye and trying to sound as grown-up as I possibly could. "You've got to promise not to tell anybody."

"Scout's honor," he said, making the sign with his fingers.

"Flip, I can use a baseball card to travel through time."

He just stared at me for a moment, as if he hadn't heard what I'd said.

"Like a time machine," I continued. "I can go back to the year on the card."

Suddenly, Flip burst out laughing, like the air exploding out of a balloon. "Oh, that's a good one, Stosh!" he moaned, holding his sides.

"You said you wouldn't laugh!"

"I can't help it!" Flip chortled, gaining control of himself.

"But I can *do* it, Flip!" I insisted. "I did it with Honus Wagner, Jackie Robinson, and Babe Ruth. If I had a Shoeless Joe Jackson card, I could go back and prevent the Black Sox Scandal from ever taking place!"

Flip burst out laughing all over again, wiping his forehead with a handkerchief. "That's what I'm gonna miss the most when the store closes," he said, shaking his head. "You kids. You kids crack me up."

"Flip, I'm serious."

"So you think you can take a Joe Jackson baseball card and it will take you back to 1919?"

"Yes!"

"Well, let me ask you this, genius. If you could really do that, why would it have to be an expensive Shoeless Joe card? Wouldn't *any* 1919 card take you back to 1919?"

I thought about that for a moment. He had a point. If all I needed was to get back to 1919, I should be able to do it with *any* card from that year.

Why hadn't I thought of that sooner?

"You're right!" I told Flip.

Flip reached into the display case and rooted around for a few seconds until he pulled out a card that was in a clear plastic sleeve. This is what it looked like:

"Who's that?"

"Heinie Groh. He played for the Cincinnati Reds. That's who the White Sox played in the 1919 Series."

"His name was *Heinie*?"

"It's a German name. Take the card, Stosh."

"How much?"

"Think of it as a present from me," he said, "for being such a good customer."

"Thanks, Flip!" I said, slipping the card into my back pocket. "Someday I'm gonna do you a favor."

"Fuhgetuhboutit," Flip said before I reached the door. "Oh, one more thing, Stosh."

"Yes?"

"Have a nice trip!" And then Flip burst out laughing again.

# 6

# Another Mission

"ABSOLUTELY NOT."

That was all my mom said when I gently brought up the idea of traveling back in time to see the 1919 World Series between the Chicago White Sox and the Cincinnati Reds. I had just come back from Flip's Fan Club, and it had seemed like Mom was in a good mood. I guess I misjudged her.

"Why not?" I asked.

"Joey," she said seriously, "you've been lucky so far. You went on a few of these adventures and nothing went wrong. But eventually something's going to happen to you. What if you got hit by a car and broke your leg? Some doctor in 1919 might want to amputate it or something. Or what if you got into trouble? They probably put kids in jail back then. And, besides, you're still getting over the flu. I'm doing this for your own good, Joey."

"That's not fair!" I complained. My nose felt like

it was running, but I didn't want her to see me wipe it. "I didn't get hurt the first three times I went to the past. And I won't get hurt if I go back again."

"The more you do it, the better the chance that something is going to go wrong."

"Actually, that's not true, Mom. If you toss a pair of dice ten times without throwing a two, that doesn't mean that you're more likely to throw a two on your next toss." (We had been studying probability in math, and I knew all about this stuff.)

"Joey, the answer is *no*."

We didn't talk much over dinner. We were both a little angry, I suppose. I was trying to think of a way to change Mom's mind when she stopped picking at her food and looked up at me.

"It was the Cincinnati Reds who were in the 1919 World Series, right?"

"Yes," I replied. "The Reds and the Chicago White Sox."

"If I let you go on this trip, would you be going to Cincinnati?"

"Well, yeah. The first game of the World Series was played in Cincinnati, so I would have to go there."

Mom went back to picking at her food for a moment. I tried to figure out why she asked me about Cincinnati.

"I had family that used to live in Cincinnati," she said softly. "It's only about a hundred miles from Louisville. My grandmother grew up there. Her name was Gladys."

"So?" I got up to scrape my plate into the trash.

"Well, I was just thinking that my grandmother was born in 1907. So in 1919 she was twelve years old."

"Your point?" I put my plate in the sink.

"Well, if you went to Cincinnati in 1919, you would be able to meet my grandmother, who was your great-grandmother."

"What?" I whined. "You want me to go visit relatives? I don't even like visiting relatives *now*, Mom! Why would I want to travel more than eighty years through time to visit my great-grandmother?"

Mom went into the living room and came back carrying an old photo album. She opened it very carefully, but little pieces of paper flaked off when she opened the faded pages. Mom had made a family tree with oval pictures of her relatives. There were dozens of aunts, uncles, and cousins going back over a hundred years. Only two ovals had no photos to go with them:

Gladys Kozinsky    Wilbur Kozinsky

"Look at this," Mom said, pointing to the empty ovals. "My grandmother Gladys and her brother Wilbur. They were twins. I never met Wilbur. He died when he was a boy. I only met my grandmother a few times at the end of her life. She was wonderful."

"How come there are no pictures of them?"

"I guess her parents didn't take many family photos after Wilbur died." My mother sighed.

Suddenly my mom got this look in her eye. A little misty-eyed, but she also had the kind of look you get when you have what you think is a brilliant idea.

"Joey," she asked, "could you take a camera back in time with you?"

"I don't know," I replied. "I never tried. I guess so."

"While you're in Cincinnati for the World Series, would you take a picture of Grandma Gladys and her brother Wilbur for me?"

I looked at my mother. A few minutes ago, she was refusing to give me permission to travel through time because it was so dangerous. Now she was *asking* me to go. Moms can be funny that way.

"I thought you were afraid I would get hurt."

"Oh, you'll be fine," Mom assured me. "You didn't get hurt the other times you went to the past, right? What could go wrong?"

I could have told her no. I had more important things to do than to go back in time and track down distant relatives so I could take snapshots of them. I had to prevent the Black Sox Scandal from happening. I had to save Shoeless Joe Jackson from a lifetime of disgrace.

But if this was what it would take for Mom to give me permission to go back in time again, I was willing.

"I'll leave tonight."

# 7

## Slipping Away

OUR HOUSE DOESN'T HAVE AN ATTIC, BUT WE DO HAVE A little storage room on the second floor where we stash stuff that would get moldy or mildewed if we kept it down in the damp basement. Mom was rooting around up there for a while before she found a box labeled KOZINSKY.

"I almost donated this stuff to charity so many times." She beamed as she brought the box downstairs to my room. "I'm glad I saved it."

She opened the box and pulled out some old clothes. Men's clothes—gray wool pants, black shoes, white shirt, suspenders, a gray hat with a small brim.

"Don't tell me," I guessed. "Wilbur Kozinsky's clothes."

"That's right," she said happily. "My grandmother's brother. That would make him your great-great uncle. Nobody in the family wanted these clothes, so I took them. I'll bet they would fit you."

"Didn't you say he died when he was a kid?" I asked, wrinkling up my nose. "Maybe he died wearing this costume."

"It's not a costume. They're *clothes*, Joey!"

"I'll look like a doofus, Mom!"

"In 1919, you'll look like the coolest kid in Cincinnati! You want to fit in, don't you? Come on, put 'em on."

I made Mom leave the room while I tried on Great-great-uncle Wilbur's clothes. Just like I thought, I looked like a doofus.

"They're too big on me," I protested when I opened the door for Mom to come back in.

"They're *perfect*," Mom said. "People wore their clothes looser back then."

"I'll bet the other kids beat him up because his name was Wilbur."

"Wilbur was probably a cool name back then, Joey. You should be happy his name wasn't Orville."

"Oh, man. I don't want to wear some dead kid's clothes."

"Oh stop it. That's silly. You look very handsome."

I didn't tell Mom, but looking at myself in the mirror, I actually thought I looked pretty sharp in Great-great-uncle Wilbur's clothes. I usually go around in the same old boring jeans and T-shirts and sneakers.

Mom found our camera in a closet in the front hallway. It's a little Olympus that would fit into my pocket. I had used the camera before. It was pretty simple. Just point and shoot. Mom loaded a roll of film into it for me.

"While you were trying on the clothes, I packed you a little lunch for tomorrow," she said, holding out a paper bag.

"No lunch!" I shouted. "I'm not bringing a dorky doggie bag with me. I can get food in 1919."

"Joey, the sanitary conditions were probably terrible in 1919. I'm sure people just threw their garbage everywhere. They had no penicillin—"

"No lunch!" I insisted.

"Okay, but take some money with you. And you have to take your medicine too. Doctor's orders."

"Okay, okay," I agreed, slipping her twenty-dollar bill and the little container of pills into my pocket.

I pretty much had everything I would need. I grabbed the Heinie Groh card, which would get me to 1919, and a pack of new baseball cards, which would bring me back home when I was ready to return.

Mom and I looked at each other awkwardly. It was always weird saying good-bye, and even weirder to think I would be going eight decades into the past.

"Can I watch?" Mom asked shyly.

"Are you sure you want to? I'm going to just disappear, you know. Vanish before your eyes. Poof! It might be creepy for you to see it happen."

"You're right." She gave me a kiss and a big hug and didn't let go for a long time. "You be careful now," she advised before closing my bedroom door. "And remember to hold the camera steady when you shoot Gladys and Wilbur."

"I will."

"Have a nice trip."

I lay down on my bed, patting my pockets to make sure I had the camera, money, and medicine. I pulled the 1919 card out of its plastic sleeve and held it in my fingertips. I thought about 1919.

I didn't know quite what to expect. World War I would be over, I knew that much. It had ended in 1918. There wouldn't be any computers or CD players or video games in 1919. I was pretty sure they would have telephones and electric lights and airplanes, though.

It wasn't long until I began to feel the tingling sensation in my fingers. It didn't hurt. It was a vibrating feeling. The hair on my arms stood on end.

I closed my eyes and thought about Cincinnati in early October, 1919. That's where I wanted to go. The baseball card—my ticket—would take me there.

The tingling moved from my fingertips to my hands and then up my arms. It seemed to linger at my shoulders for a moment before washing up over my face and down my chest like a wave. I tried to wiggle my toes, but they wouldn't wiggle.

And then, like a movie screen fading into white, I felt my body slipping away.

# 8

# Don't Bet on It

WHEN I OPENED MY EYES, I WAS SITTING ON A TOILET bowl. It obviously wasn't anybody's house. The walls were made of cinder blocks, and the bathroom was dirty. Lining the walls were metal shelves filled with cleaning supplies and junk. The bathroom was lit by a single bare lightbulb that was dangling from the ceiling by a wire. The door was closed.

I patted my pockets to make sure the camera, money, and medicine were still with me. They were. I had my baseball cards, too.

There was a newspaper on the floor—*The Cincinnati Bugle*. The date at the top of the front page was September 30, 1919. Perfect. I was at the right place and the right time. Everything was going exactly as I had planned so far. I couldn't help but smile when I saw how much the newspaper cost—two cents.

I scanned the front page, and my eye was quickly caught by the main story.

September 30, 1919

# WORLD SERIES TO BEGIN TOMORROW

### Sox heavily favored to triumph over Reds

*Special to The Cincinnati Bugle*

**CINCINNATI, Sept. 29** — Baseball's Golden Jubilee In Redland will be celebrated with the opening of the world's series tomorrow, when our Cincinnati club, champions of the National League, will clash with the Chicago White Sox, the pennant winners of the American League. A multitudinous array of Cincinnati partisans are expected to turn out at Redland Park, this being the first year the local nine has reached the grand finale of baseball season.

I couldn't believe everything was going so smoothly. On my previous trips to the past, something always seemed to go wrong. I would end up in a different city than the one I wanted to go to, or I'd find myself lost in a dark alley or something. I never seemed to wind up exactly where I wanted to be. Maybe this time I'd done everything right.

Next to the article about the World Series was another article that caught my eye.

# TWENTY MILLION PERISHED IN 1918 INFLUENZA EPIDEMIC!

### Special to the Cincinnati Bugle

Even **THE GREAT WAR,** which killed more than nine million soldiers, was dwarfed by last year's influenza scourge. **500,000 AMERICANS** and over **TWENTY MILLION PEOPLE** around the world were lost to the mysterious virus. No infection, war, or famine ever killed so many in such a short period of time. No cause or cure has been found for the disease, and nobody knows if it might

*The Great War.* That must have been what they called World War I back then. Of course, that made sense. They wouldn't call it World War I because they didn't know that there would ever be a World War II.

I had no idea there was any worldwide plague in 1918. Between World War I and the influenza epidemic, as many as twenty-nine million people died in a very short amount of time. I wondered how many people there were in the *world* in 1918. A big chunk of the earth's population must have been wiped out by war and disease.

But I had other things on my mind. I had to get to Shoeless Joe Jackson and convince him not to throw the World Series.

There was a clicking noise above my head. I put my ear to the door and heard a familiar sound—the clicking of one billiard ball striking another one. I must be in the bathroom of a pool parlor, I guessed.

Cautiously, I opened the door and was grateful that it didn't squeak. The room was pretty dark. It looked like a basement. There was a row of wooden shelves next to the bathroom that separated it from the rest of the room. More junk was on the shelves. I could hear voices at the other side of the room.

"Is Jackson in on it?" a gruff man's voice asked.

"Not yet, A.R.," another guy replied.

"We gotta get Jackson in."

They could be talking about Shoeless Joe Jackson, I concluded. I peered through the junk on the shelves, being careful not to make a sound.

Three guys were sitting around a table, about fifteen feet away from me. One of them was overweight, and he was dressed in a plain dark suit and tie. He had a mustache. The other two guys were thin and wore hats. It looked like the fat guy they called A.R. was their boss. All three puffed on cigars. The room stunk. I knew the smoke wasn't good for my sinuses, and I hoped it wouldn't make me sneeze. I wiped my nose on my sleeve.

What grabbed my attention was not the three guys but the table they were sitting around. It was covered, every square inch of it, with money. Stacks of bills, four or five inches thick, were rubber-banded together and piled on top of one another until they were toppling over. I couldn't tell if they were five-dollar bills or tens or hundreds or what. But even if they were one-dollar bills, it was a tremendous amount of cash. More than I had ever seen in my life, that was for sure.

I didn't think the three guys were drug dealers. I wasn't even sure if there *were* drugs in 1919. They must be crooks, I concluded.

"We got the two best pitchers in," one of the skinny guys explained. "Lefty Williams is in. Eddie Cicotte is in." The guy pronounced "Cicotte" like "see cot."

"Risberg's in too," the other skinny guy said. "And Chick Gandil and McMullin—"

"That ain't good enough, Billy!" A.R. said, raising his voice. "Jackson hit .351 this year. He could get hot, blow the Series wide open, and I lose a bundle. I want Jackson in or the deal's off."

I couldn't believe it. Of all the places for me to land! These were the gamblers who were planning the World Series fix! If they found out I was listening to them . . . I didn't want to think about what might happen.

I wiped my nose on my sleeve again and silently slipped my camera out of my pocket. A picture of these guys might be important to have later on. Carefully, I braced the camera against the shelf and found the guy they called A.R. in the viewfinder. I snapped the shutter.

*Bzzzzzzzz.*

Shoot! I had forgotten that the camera made a buzzing sound as it advanced the film for the next shot.

**Carefully, I braced the camera against the shelf and found the guy they called A.R. in the viewfinder. I snapped the shutter.**

"What was that?" the skinny guy named Billy asked suddenly.

"What was *what*?"

"I heard a click and a buzz."

Quickly, I slipped the camera back into my pocket and held my breath.

"It was nothin'," the other skinny guy said, "just the pool tables upstairs."

I exhaled.

"Relax," A.R. told Billy. "Look, Comiskey only pays Jackson somethin' like six grand a year. Offer him ten grand and I bet he plays ball with us."

"You kiddin'?" the other skinny guy said. "Six thousand a year for a star like Joe Jackson? I make more 'n that, and I sure can't hit .351."

"A crime, ain't it?" A.R. chuckled. "Comiskey even makes the players pay him to wash their uniforms. That's how cheap he is."

The three of them laughed. My legs were getting tired from staying motionless for so long. I took advantage of the noise they were making to shift my weight from one foot to the other.

The smoke from their cigars was starting to get to me. My eyes were watering. I wiped my nose on my sleeve again. I looked around. I had to find a way to get out of there without them noticing me.

"What if Jackson don't take the ten grand?" Billy asked A.R.

"Offer him twenty grand. If that don't work . . . well, you know how to persuade people, don'tcha, Abe?"

The skinny guy named Abe smiled and pumped his right fist into the palm of his left hand twice.

"Jackson's got a pretty young wife, don't he?" Billy asked.

"I'm sure he wouldn't want anything to happen to her," A.R. said, which made Abe and Billy laugh some more.

"Of course, we don't work that way," A.R. told them, "unless it's absolutely necessary."

"And they said nobody could fix da World Series." Billy chuckled.

"I coulda fixed the war if there was any money in it," A.R. replied.

Billy and Abe laughed again and got up from the table as if they were going to leave.

"So do we have a deal, Mr. Rothstein?" Abe asked. Now I knew that the *R* in A.R. stood for "Rothstein."

"One more thing, boys," Rothstein said. "I want a signal in the first inning of the first game. I need to see a sign that the fix is on."

"What kinda sign?"

"Tell Cicotte to hit the first Cincinnati batter with a pitch. When I see that, I'll know the players are . . . cooperating."

"No problem, Mr. Rothstein. I'll tell Cicotte."

"So can we have the eighty grand?" Abe asked, eyeing the money on the table. "The players want to get paid before they lose the first game."

"I don't care *what* the players want," Rothstein replied, picking up one small stack of bills from all the piles on the table. "I need this cash to get down on bets. Here's ten grand for Cicotte to lose the first game and ten to pay Jackson to make sure he's in. Tell the rest they'll get paid twenty grand after each game the Sox lose."

"They're gonna be mad, A.R. I promised 'em they'd get paid eighty grand in *advance*."

"So what are they gonna do?" Rothstein asked with a smile. "Call the cops?"

The three of them scooped the money off the table and into a big cardboard box. In another minute or so, they would be gone and I could sneak out of there without them knowing I'd heard every word they'd said.

The haze of smoke just about filled the room now, and I could feel it in my nose and throat. I turned my head and swallowed, taking a deep breath. If I could just hold my breath until they were gone, I'd be okay.

And then I coughed.

"What was that?" Rothstein asked quickly, turning toward the shelves I was standing behind.

# 9

## The Bad Old Days

THERE WAS NO PLACE TO HIDE. ABE AND BILLY WERE ON me in seconds, grabbing my arms and twisting them behind my back. Rothstein stood in front and looked me over.

"What's your name, kid?"

"J-Joe Stoshack."

"Who sent you?" he asked calmly.

"Nobody sent me," I replied honestly. "I . . . sent myself."

"What are you doing here?"

"I . . . was just using the bathroom . . ."

"What did you hear?"

"Nothing."

"He's just a stupid little kid, A.R.," Billy said.

"But what if he's a *smart* little kid?" Rothstein wondered out loud. "Maybe he heard everything we were saying. We can't have him blabbing."

"I won't blab!" I said, but they ignored me.

"You want me to search him?" Billy asked, tightening his grip on my arm.

I swallowed hard. I didn't care about my medicine, but if these guys found my camera in my pocket, there would be no telling what they might do to me. And if they took my baseball cards, there would be no way for me to ever get back home. I would be stuck in 1919 forever. My nose was dripping, but I couldn't do anything about it.

"Nah," Rothstein replied, and I relaxed a little.

"I bet if I bust his face up a little he won't blab," Abe remarked. I swallowed again.

"Shut up, Abe," Rothstein snapped.

"I didn't hear anything, sir," I whined. "I swear I didn't."

Rothstein leaned over and slipped a key into Billy's hand, whispering something into his ear. Billy nodded his head.

"These men are not going to hurt you, sonny," Rothstein said to me, like a kindly uncle. "But I don't like to take risks, and I can't take the risk that you can keep your mouth shut for the next twenty-four hours. So if you just do everything these men tell you to do, you'll be fine. You understand me?"

"Yes, sir."

Billy and Abe led me up some rickety wooden stairs into the billiard parlor. A bunch of men were shooting pool and smoking. None of them paid any attention to me.

"I'm gonna loosen my grip on your arm," Abe whispered in my ear. "But if you get away, Mr. Rothstein will be very mad at me. So if you try to run, I'm gonna have to hurt you. Got that?"

"Yes."

I believed every word he said. These guys looked like the kind of guys whose solution to most problems would be to hurt somebody.

"Just walk next to me, kid."

They marched me through the poolroom and out the front door into the street. It was buzzing with activity. Old-time cars—they looked like Model Ts to me—were chugging all over, spewing exhaust. There were trolleys, too, and horse-drawn buggies.

People—mostly men—clogged the sidewalks, hurrying to who knew where. All of them were wearing hats. A sign on a little grocery store window said MILK—15 CENTS A QUART.

For once in my life I was glad I'd taken my mother's advice. Dressed as I was, I fit right in. The few women I saw were wearing long dresses and hats. In the snippets of conversations I was able to catch, everybody seemed to be talking about the World Series.

"—Reds are gonna murder the Sox tomorrow!"

"—They'd better. I put my money on 'em."

"—Sox won it all in '17."

"—Reds haven't been in the Series, ever."

**Old-time cars—they looked like Model Ts to me—were chugging all over, spewing exhaust. There were trolleys, too, and horse-drawn buggies.**

"—Sox are favored . . ."

"—Cicotte is a pretty good hurler . . ."

Abe and Billy walked me a block down the street. I tried to pay close attention to everything, in case I would need to retrace my steps later. They led me through a big set of double doors and into a building. Over the door was a sign that read SINTON HOTEL.

The lobby was jammed with people, again mostly men. Many of them were shouting, and some of them were even standing on chairs waving money in the air. As we walked through, I saw a guy with a fistful of money.

"A thousand bucks says the Sox win by at least three runs tomorrow!"

"I'll take that bet!" replied another guy.

"Who will give me even money on the Reds?"

"The odds are seven to five!"

"Suckers." Abe snickered as he pushed me through the crowd. He and Billy led me through a door that opened onto a stairway. They led me upstairs.

"Who is Mr. Rothstein?" I asked, comfortable enough now to feel like they were not about to kill me.

"None of your business," Billy said. "You're lucky Mr. R. didn't tell us to hurt you. He ain't the type of man who likes to hurt things. Let's just say that Mr. R. is a man who likes to fix things."

"Yeah," added Abe. "Things that ain't broke."

"Shut up, Abe."

It seemed pretty obvious that this Rothstein guy was the boss of Billy and Abe, and Billy was the boss of Abe, and Abe was the boss of me. We reached the third floor of the hotel, and they took me down the hall. They stopped at Room 313. Billy pulled out the key that Rothstein had given him and opened the door.

The hotel room was empty. I mean, there was a bed in there and all, but no suitcases or anything. Nobody was staying there. It looked pretty nice. If I had to stay there for twenty-four hours with one of them guarding me, it wouldn't be the worst thing that had ever happened to me.

"Whose room is this?" Abe asked Billy.

"Heinie Groh," Billy replied, "but he ain't usin' it."

Heinie Groh! *I never should have taken that Heinie Groh baseball card*, I thought to myself. Billy opened the door to a closet.

"Get in," he ordered.

"I have to stay in the closet?" I asked.

"Whaddaya complainin' about?" Abe remarked, giving me a shove. "This is the best hotel in town."

The closet was completely empty except for a few wire hangers on a rod. I stepped inside. It was pretty small, about the size of a phone booth. I had to duck my head so I wouldn't bump into the rod.

"We'll come get you out after the game tomorrow," Billy said, as he reached into his jacket pocket. He pulled out a Hershey bar and flipped it into the closet. "This oughta hold you till then."

Then he closed the closet door. I heard a lock click, and a few seconds later the hotel room door clicked shut, too.

I put my ear to the door. Silence. They were gone.

I was in total darkness. I felt around the door for the doorknob. Maybe I could break the lock or pick it or something. But there *was* no doorknob. The closet door was locked from the other side, probably with a bolt or latch. I leaned against the door and tried bumping my shoulder into it. The door was solid. It wasn't going anywhere. I was stuck.

I sank down to the closet floor and sat there. Why did this always have to happen to *me*? I had come to 1919 to try and do something good. All I wanted to do was warn Shoeless Joe Jackson about ruining his life. I hadn't even *found* Shoeless Joe, and it didn't look like I was going to, sitting in a locked closet.

Why is it that every time I decide to take a trip back to "the good old days," something goes wrong and I run into trouble?

My nose was running, my eyes were watering, my throat felt tight, and it took me a few seconds even to realize that it wasn't because I had the flu. It was because I was crying.

Hungry. I was hungry, too, I realized. My stomach was rumbling. If only I had listened to my mother and brought along the lunch she had packed for me. Oh, it wouldn't have mattered. Those guys Billy and Abe probably would have taken it away from me anyway.

I felt around the floor of the closet until my hands found the Hershey bar. Tearing off the wrapper, I took a little nibble. If I ate a little bit every hour, I figured, maybe it would last me the whole day and night.

Oh, forget about that. I scarfed the whole thing down in two bites. It tasted great but didn't make me feel any better about the situation I was in.

My eyes were starting to adjust to the dark, and

I could see a narrow slit of light under the door. I couldn't do anything about it, but that sliver of light was comforting in a way. At least it told me it wasn't nighttime yet. There was nothing to do but think.

I couldn't escape. I could sit there and wait it out until those creeps came to get me again. And who knew what they were going to do with me *then*? They knew I'd overheard them planning the World Series fix. They would have to keep me quiet for the entire Series so they could make their money betting against the White Sox without me "blabbing." Maybe they would decide it would be easier to just kill me so they wouldn't have to worry about me anymore.

And if they killed me, who would know? My mother wouldn't even be *born* until the 1960s.

Suddenly, another thought occurred to me. I didn't have to sit there and do nothing. I had the pack of baseball cards in my pocket. I could get out of the closet whenever I wanted to. I could use my new cards and travel back to my own time. I didn't have to alert Shoeless Joe Jackson. I could go home to my own house, my own bed, my own mom. I could be safe.

Obviously, that was the smart solution. I tore open the pack of new cards, holding one of them in my hand and slipping the others back inside my pocket. I closed my eyes and thought about going home.

Just as the first tingling sensation tickled my fingertips, there was a voice.

"Cheap Commy."

The voice was coming from the back of the closet, the opposite side away from the door. It must be coming from the room next to the room I was locked in. Somebody was in there.

"Yer out, busher."

There it was again. A mysterious voice.

I let the card slip from my fingers. The tingling sensation stopped.

# 10

## Room with a View

I COULDN'T TELL IF THE VOICE COMING FROM THE NEXT room was male or female, but it didn't matter. Somebody was there and that somebody could get me out of the closet I had been locked in.

"Hey!" I shouted, putting my mouth against the back wall of the closet. "Can you hear me?"

No response.

"Help!" I screamed, pounding the wall. "I'm locked in the closet of the room next door! Get me out, will you?"

Nothing.

"What are you, deaf?" I hollered.

Then it occurred to me that maybe there *was* a deaf person in the room next door. Why else wouldn't somebody respond?

As I leaned on the back wall of the closet, my finger brushed against something sharp. I ran my fingers all over the wall until I found the spot again. It was a screw. The back panel of the closet was held on by screws!

Excitedly, I felt around until I found the screw in each corner of the wall. If I could loosen the screws, maybe I could remove the panel and get out of there.

I didn't have a screwdriver or anything, but I felt in my pockets to see if anything could serve the same purpose. All I had was my camera, a twenty-dollar bill, my baseball cards, and the container of medicine.

I felt around on the floor. I couldn't see anything, so I slid my hands all over, trying to cover every inch. After a few minutes, my hand felt something. It was a coin. I could tell it was a dime because the edges were ridged. Perfect.

The dime fit into the head of the screw. *Righty tighty, lefty loosey*, I remembered. The screw didn't turn easily, but it did turn. I was able to slowly remove the top left screw from the wall. Three more to go.

"Cheap Commy."

There it was again! The voice. What did "cheap Commy" mean? I pounded the wall.

"Who's Commy?" I yelled. "Push the wall out!"

No response. Whoever it was in the next room was starting to get on my nerves. I decided to forget about the voice and just get all four screws out. It didn't matter who was on the other side. All that mattered was that I would get out of there.

It took about ten minutes to get the second screw out of the wall. Dimes are not made to be used as screwdrivers, and my fingers were tired. I didn't look forward to spending twenty minutes to remove the bottom two screws.

I pulled on the panel on the off chance that it might come off with two screws still attached. Surprisingly, it pulled away from the wall. I gave it a good pull, and the bottom two screws ripped right out. The board fell off and bumped to the floor.

I expected there would be light behind the board from the room next door, but it was pitch-black. I stepped through the opening, and my foot landed on a shoe. Feeling around with my other foot, I could feel shoes all over the place. That was when I realized that I had broken out of my closet and was now in the closet of the room next door.

"Commy's a crook," the voice repeated, a little more clearly now.

"Oh, hush, sweetie," a woman's voice said. "Is that any way to say hello?"

"Commy's a crook," the voice said.

Now there are *two* of them! I froze. This could be a sticky situation, it occurred to me. If I pushed open their closet door and they found me in there, they might freak out. They might think I broke into their room. They might call the police or hotel security. They might arrest me for breaking and entering.

Frantically, I began to think of something I could say that would prepare them for the fact that there was a strange kid in their closet.

*"Excuse me, ma'am, I'm in serious trouble."*

*"Miss, I don't mean to alarm you but—"*

*"Please don't be afraid. I was locked in the room next door—"*

But I never got the chance to say any of those things. Just before I was going to speak, the closet door opened from the other side.

A woman, about twenty-five, was standing in front of me.

She was totally naked.

"Eeeeeeeeeeeeeeeeeeeeeeeeeeeeek!" she screamed.

Right behind her, on the dresser, was a big birdcage.

"Commy's a crook," the bird squawked. "Cheap Commy."

# 11

## Katie and Joe

"EEEEEEEEEEEEEEEEEEEEEEEEEEEEEEEEK!"

Without thinking, I put my hands over my eyes. My face must have been red as a fire engine. The lady standing in front of me grabbed a bathrobe from the hook on the closet door and quickly wrapped it around herself. I guess I don't look all that frightening, because she seemed to relax almost immediately. She looked at me curiously. It was as if she was wondering how I could have possibly gotten into her closet. And why.

The lady was pretty, with pale blue eyes and brown hair that sort of swirled up around her head. Glancing out the window, I could see that it was dark outside. I had been locked in that closet for a long time.

Suddenly, a guy charged out of the bathroom waving a black wooden baseball bat.

**The lady was pretty, with pale blue eyes and brown hair that sort of swirled up around her head.**

"You okay, Katie?" he shouted. He had a thick Southern accent. When he saw me cowering in the closet, he waved the bat around menacingly. "Ah'll kill 'im! Just say the word, Katie, and Ah'll split his head like a melon!"

I put my arms up in self-defense and took a step backward. The guy's dark brown eyes were on fire. He was a tall man, over six feet, with short, coal-black hair that was parted in the middle and flattened down. You might call him handsome if you saw him, except for the fact that his ears stuck out a little too far. He was wearing boxer shorts. He was thin but had very long, thick arms.

"He's just a boy, Joe," the lady named Katie said calmly. "Leave him be."

"Commy's a crook," the bird said.

"Shut yer trap!" the guy named Joe yelled at the bird, waving the bat around.

As the bat hovered a few inches from my face, I noticed some letters carved into it. I squinted so I could read them.

## BETSY

That's when I realized that the lunatic waving the bat around was no ordinary Joe. And it was no ordinary bat. That bat must be the famous Black Betsy. And if that was Black Betsy, the lunatic waving it around was just the man I wanted to see.

"A-are you . . . Shoeless Joe Jackson?" I asked, holding my hands over my face in case he was still thinking about splitting my head open.

The guy stiffened, like I'd said the wrong thing.

"Please don't call him that," Katie advised me.

"Ah hate that name," Joe said, placing the bat carefully on the bed. He seemed to have calmed down a little, talking slowly in a deep Southern drawl. "Ah ain't some dumb country bumpkin. See for yourself. Ah got plenty of shoes."

The closet I was still standing in was filled with shoes, many of them men's.

"I'm sorry, sir," I apologized.

"Just call me Joe."

"My name is Joe, too," I said, extending a hand hesitantly and stepping out of the closet. "Joe Stoshack. Most folks call me Stosh."

"Pleased to meetcha, Stosh," Joe said, taking my hand in a muscular grip. "This here's my wife, Katie."

I wasn't sure if Joe knew I'd seen his wife with no clothes on, and I wasn't about to tell him. I shook her hand, too, a little embarrassed.

"What're ya doin' hidin' in my closet for, boy?" Joe asked. "You an autograph seeker? Katie, make this boy Stosh one of my signatures the way you do so nicely, will you please, honey?"

"No," I said, stopping Katie before she could get a pen. "I didn't come for an autograph. Mr. Jackson, I came here to give you an important message."

"What might that be?" Joe asked, smiling as if to say no message delivered by a kid could be of much importance to him.

"Don't take the money!" I urged him. "It will ruin your life! You'll be banned from baseball forever. You've got to believe me!"

"Whoa!" Joe said, chuckling. "Slow down, son. What money? Ah don't know what you're talkin' 'bout."

"The World Series is fixed!" I informed him. "I overheard some gamblers. They're paying some of the players on the White Sox to lose on purpose. Then they're going to bet against the Sox and make a fortune for themselves."

Joe threw back his head and laughed.

"That's crazy talk," Katie said.

"Nobody could fix the Series." Joe chuckled. "They'd have to pay off seven or eight guys, a coupla startin' pitchers—"

"They *did*!" I insisted. "I heard them. Eddie

Cicotte and Lefty Williams are in on the fix. And they plan to get you in on it, too."

"Well, Ah ain't *gonna* be in on it."

"Cheap cheap," the bird chirped. "Cheap Commy."

"Ah don't care how cheap Commy is," Joe said. "Ah wouldn't do that. That's plain wrong. Ah play to win. That's the only way Ah know how to play."

"Who's Commy?" I asked.

"Charles Comiskey," Katie told me, "the guy who owns the Sox."

The phone rang. It wasn't the kind of ring I was used to back home. Our phone at home rang sort of like *tootle*. This one sounded like a little jangly bell. Joe's wife picked it up. It was one of those black phones I'd seen in old movies, where you pick the whole phone up in one hand and then hold the little receiver to your ear with your other hand.

"It's Eddie Cicotte," Katie said, glancing at me before handing the phone to Joe.

Joe listened for a few seconds, shaking his head. He looked over at me, too.

"Ah want no part of that," was all he said before hanging up.

"What did he want?" Katie asked.

Joe sat down on the bed, a dazed look on his face. "Eddie said he'd give me ten thousand bucks to help the boys kick the Series."

Katie sat down on the bed next to Joe. "*Ten thousand dollars?*" she said, awed. "Joe, that's more than you earn all *season*."

Joe turned to me suddenly. "How'd you know that was gonna happen?"

I wasn't sure if I should tell Joe and Katie that I came from the future and knew all about the Black Sox Scandal. They might think I was crazy or something.

"Like I told you," I said. "I overheard some gamblers talking about it."

"Ten . . . thousand . . . dollars," Katie repeated. It occurred to me that in 1919, ten thousand dollars might sound like a million. "We could sure use ten thousand dollars."

"Don't do it, Joe," I warned.

"*Course* Ah'm not gonna do it," he snapped.

Joe got up off the bed and grabbed Black Betsy with his right hand. He stood in the middle of the room and held the bat outstretched, his arm perfectly straight. The end of the bat nearly reached the wall. He closed his eyes and stood like a statue.

"You want me to send the boy away, Joe?" Katie asked.

"He can stay if he wants."

"What's he doing?" I whispered to Katie.

"That's how he relaxes and gets ready for a game," she replied. "It keeps his muscles strong."

"How long does he hold the bat out like that?"

"A half hour," she replied. "Then he'll switch to the other hand."

Once I was in science class and Mr. Kane wanted to show us how our muscles worked. He asked us to take a book in one hand and hold it out in front of us. He had a stopwatch and he called out the seconds. In fifteen seconds my arm was sore. In thirty seconds it was really hurting. After one minute, I had to drop the book because I couldn't take the pain anymore. Most of the kids in the class didn't even make it to thirty seconds.

Joe just stood there calmly, holding the bat— bigger than any bat I'd ever seen—like it was a feather. His arm wasn't even trembling.

"You hungry?" Katie asked, holding out a brown paper bag. "We have some leftovers from dinner."

I suddenly realized I was starving. I took the bag thankfully and pulled out a piece of steak.

"How about a drink?"

"Do you have a can of Coke?" I asked.

Katie and Joe looked at me strangely, and I knew I had made a mistake. Maybe Coke hadn't been invented yet.

"You . . . uh . . . don't have Coke?" I asked.

"Oh, we have Coke," Katie replied.

"But it don't come in *cans*." Joe chuckled.

Katie looked at me suspiciously, but she handed me a bottle of Coke and used a little metal can opener to pry the top off. Then she grabbed a towel from a drawer and went into the bathroom. Joe kept holding the bat up.

"Is it okay if I talk to you while you do that, Mr. Jackson?"

"If it pleases you."

"Say a player *did* want to lose a game on

purpose," I asked. "How could he do it without anybody knowing?"

"Easy," Joe replied. "He could get a late jump runnin' for a fly ball. Then he could dive for the ball and miss it by an inch. He'd look like he was tryin', but all he did was turn an out into a triple. There's other ways. He could make his throws slightly off target. Hittin', he could swing a little late. There's a million ways to lose a ball game if you set your mind to it."

Beads of sweat were starting to form on Joe's face, but the bat didn't droop or shake. He held it out steadily. I heard Katie brushing her teeth in the bathroom.

"Where are you from, Stosh?" Joe asked me.

"Louisville, Kentucky."

"You don't say?" Joe replied, smiling with his eyes still closed. "Ah'm a South Carolina boy. Born and raised in Greenville, just a coupla hundred miles from you. You came all the way to Cincinnati from Louisville?"

"I guess you could say that," I replied.

I wasn't afraid Joe was going to brain me with Black Betsy anymore. We were getting downright chummy. I was relieved that he showed no interest in taking money to throw the World Series.

"Mr. Jackson," I asked, "how come they call you Shoeless Joe?"

Joe grimaced. The bat was beginning to shake a little.

"Ah was just startin' out in the minors." He

grunted. "And one day my new spikes was givin' me blisters. They hurt so bad Ah couldn't put 'em on. The manager wouldn't let me sit out the game. So Ah took off my spikes and went to the outfield in my stockin' feet. Some reporter noticed and he called me Shoeless Joe in the paper the next day. That was all it took."

"You only did it that one time?"

"Sometimes you do just one dumb thing in your life and that's all anybody remembers about you."

Joe was really struggling now to keep holding the bat up. His face was twisted with pain and wet with sweat. He was breathing heavily. I didn't want to distract him anymore. Katie came out of the bathroom.

"Do you have a TV in here?" I asked her.

"TV?" she asked, puzzled.

"Television."

"Television?"

Suddenly I realized my stupid mistake. There was no television in 1919. Looking around the room, I didn't even see a radio. That probably hadn't been invented yet either. I had to think fast.

"I meant, can I use the telephone," I said abruptly.

Joe lowered the bat with a gasp and rubbed his shoulder. He and Katie looked at each other. Joe nodded. He picked up Black Betsy in his other hand and held it out in front of him.

I didn't really need to use the telephone. But it

was the first thing I thought of when I realized television hadn't been invented. I picked up the phone and held the receiver to my ear the way Katie and Joe did.

"How do you dial this thing?" I asked.

"Dial?" Katie asked. "What do you mean, dial?"

Joe and Katie looked at me strangely. Oh no. I'd made another stupid mistake! Telephones must not have had dials or keypads in 1919. Now I was really in trouble. I felt like a jerk.

"Just tell the operator who you want to talk to," Katie instructed.

"Ain'tcha never used a telephone before?" Joe asked with a snort. "And they say *Ah'm* dumb!"

"The, uh . . . the phones in Louisville are different," I explained lamely.

I didn't go any further, because a woman's voice came on the line.

"Cincinnati operator," she announced pleasantly.

"Hello," I replied.

"What can I do for you?" the operator asked.

"Uh . . ."

Joe and Katie were staring at me, like they didn't quite know what to make of me.

"Do you wish to speak with someone?" the operator asked.

I searched my brain for a response. I had to make the call look real. If Katie and Joe found out I was a fraud, they'd probably throw me out of the room.

That's when I remembered that I *did* have to make a phone call. There *was* somebody in Cincinnati I wanted to speak to. I struggled to remember the name.

"Kozinsky," I told the operator. "I would like to speak with Gladys Kozinsky."

# 12

## An Offer

WHEN I TOLD THE OPERATOR THAT I WANTED TO SPEAK with Gladys Kozinsky, I was pretty sure she was going to tell me there was no such person. Or she would tell me she couldn't make the connection or the number was unlisted or something. Or maybe Gladys Kozinsky wouldn't be home. I really doubted that my great-grandmother Gladys was going to pick up the phone.

But the operator *did* have a listing of one Kozinsky in Cincinnati, and I asked her to connect me. After a few seconds of clicks and scratchy noises, a boy's muffled voice came on the line.

"Hello?"

"Uh," I said, "is Gladys Kozinsky home?"

"Who wants to know?" the boy asked.

"My name is Joe," I told him. "Joe Stoshack."

The phone clattered, like it had been dropped on the floor.

"Gladys!" the kid hollered. "There's somebody on the phone for you . . . and it's a *boy!*" He giggled. I heard footsteps and then a few seconds of arguing. One of them must have put a hand over the mouthpiece, but I thought I heard a girl's voice say, "Shut up, Wilbur," and his reply, "*You* shut up."

"Hello?" a girl said sweetly.

"Is this Gladys Kozinsky from Cincinnati?" I asked.

"Yes, it is. Who is this?"

I took a deep breath and paused for a moment to appreciate how amazing it was. I was actually *speaking* with my great-grandmother, who had died many years before I was born.

"My name is Joe Stoshack."

"Joe who?"

"Stoshack."

"Do you go to my school?"

"No . . ."

"Then how do you know me?"

I hadn't counted on actually reaching my great-grandmother, so I hadn't given much thought to what I would say if I *did* reach her. I couldn't tell her that I had come from the future or that we were related, of course. But I had to come up with some reason for calling her up.

I looked around the hotel room. Joe Jackson was holding the bat up in his other hand and his wife was brushing her hair.

"You and your brother are twins, right?" I asked Gladys.

"Yes . . ."

"I need to take a picture of twins."

"A photograph?" she asked.

"Yes."

"Why?"

"It's . . . for a school project," I lied. "Would you mind letting me take a pic—photograph—of you and your brother?"

She didn't say anything for a moment, then replied simply, "I guess so."

"When can we shoot the picture?" I asked.

"Well, are you going to the game tomorrow?"

"You mean the World Series?"

"Of *course* I mean the World Series!" she said. "What other game could I be talking about?"

"I'll be there."

"My parents always let us go buy hot dogs after the fourth inning," she explained. "You can meet us at the hot dog stand on the third-base side. Okay?"

"Okay!"

There was a loud knock at the hotel room door. Somebody said, "Jackson, you in there?"

I was afraid it was one of the gamblers who had locked me in the closet. Joe and Katie looked at each other, then they looked at me. Joe put the bat down and put on a bathrobe. Then he picked up Black Betsy with both hands.

"Get in the bathroom!" Katie whispered to me urgently.

"I gotta go," I told Gladys. "See you tomorrow." I hung up the phone and rushed into the bathroom.

After closing the door, I got down on my knees and peeked through the keyhole.

"Hiya, Chick," I heard Joe say, after letting somebody into the room. I remembered that the gamblers had mentioned that a player named Chick was in on the fix.

Looking through the keyhole, I could see that Chick Gandil was a really big guy, taller than Joe and at least two hundred pounds. He had hollow cheeks and he was puffing a cigar. He took off his hat when he saw Joe's wife. Gandil was dressed neatly in a sports jacket.

"Evenin', Mrs. Jackson," he said politely. Chick Gandil didn't have a Southern accent like Joe and Katie. "Getting some last-minute batting practice in, Joe?"

"What do you want, Chick?" Joe asked. It didn't look like he liked Gandil.

Chick threw an enormous arm around Joe's shoulder. "Joe, a bunch of us got together and we decided to frame up the Series. Eddie Cicotte told me you weren't interested in helping us."

"That's right, Chick," Joe said, breaking away from Gandil's arm. "Ah play to win. That's the way Ah do things."

"You're a fine man, Joe," Gandil continued, "but the men we're working with want you in this thing pretty badly. They told me they would pay you twenty thousand dollars if necessary. Four payments of five thousand each."

Katie gasped loudly enough so I could hear it through the bathroom door, even though I couldn't see her through the keyhole.

"The answer is *no*, Chick," Joe said firmly. "Ah get money to win games, not lose 'em."

Gandil didn't turn and leave, as I expected him to. He turned toward Katie.

"Mrs. Jackson," he said, "maybe you can talk some sense into your husband. Maybe Joe doesn't quite understand how much money we're talking about here. You can buy a lot of pretty things for yourself with twenty grand."

"Joe knows exactly how much money you're talking about," Katie snapped. "Joe makes up his own mind."

"Get out of here, Chick," Joe said, gripping Black Betsy.

"Look," Gandil persisted, "the fix is on, Joe. It's gonna happen with you or without you. Even if you hit four homers tomorrow, Eddie Cicotte is gonna lose the game. You might as well cash in like the rest of us."

"That don't matter to me."

Joe had Black Betsy on his shoulder and took a step toward Chick.

"We'll lose no matter how good you play, Joe," Chick said, taking a step backward.

"Then Ah'll have to play better," Joe said, taking another step toward the big man.

"Joe, I shouldn't be telling you this, but we

already told the gamblers you're in on it so they wouldn't back out of the deal. You might as well—"

"Ah said *no!*"

Joe took a swing at Chick with Black Betsy. Gandil bailed out like it was a high, inside fastball. The bat missed his head by less than an inch.

"Fine!" Chick said, backing out the door. "You play your game and I'll play mine!"

Joe slammed the door. I came out of the bathroom. Katie began to sob and Joe went over and hugged her.

"Ah'm sorry, honey," he said, stroking her hair. "Ah know that money would be nice, but—"

"It's not that," Katie whimpered. "You've been working hard all season. All the fellas have. You're the best team in baseball. I know how much you wanted to win the Series."

"Ah'll win it anyways," Joe said. "Ah don't care how many of 'em lay down."

Suddenly, the hotel room door opened again. Chick Gandil was back.

"Who's the kid?" he asked, startled to see me suddenly standing there.

"My nephew," Joe said, "from Louisville. What do you want now?"

Chick reached into his jacket pocket. For a second I thought he might be reaching for a gun. Instead, he pulled out a thick envelope.

"They told me to give you this no matter what,"

he said, flipping the envelope onto the bed. "You can do what you want with it."

Gandil backed out the door and shut it behind him.

**"They told me to give you this no matter what," he said, flipping the envelope onto the bed. "You can do what you want with it."**

# 13

# Dirty Money

WHEN CHICK GANDIL THREW THE ENVELOPE ON THE bed, the flap opened up a little, and some bills slid out. Twenties. Fifties. Hundred-dollar bills. When Gandil left, Joe and Katie just stared at the envelope, like it had a contagious disease and they didn't want to touch it. Finally, Katie picked up the envelope and counted the money.

"Five . . . thousand . . . dollars," she said, whistling in wonder and flapping the bills in the air. "I've never seen so much money in one place at one time."

Joe locked the hotel room door. He didn't want any more uninvited guests. He didn't seem interested in holding the money in his hand.

"Ah don't play ball for money," he said softly. "Ah play ball to win. Ah would play ball for free. That money is filthy."

"What should we do with it, Joe?" Katie asked.

"Beats me."

"You've got to report it to the commissioner of baseball!" I exclaimed. "If you tell him how you got the money, he can't blame you when word gets out that the Sox threw the Series! He won't ban you from the game for the rest of your life!"

Joe and Katie looked at me blankly.

"What's a commissioner?" Katie asked me.

"There's no commissioner of baseball?" I asked weakly.

They both shook their heads. That's when I realized that the first baseball commissioner took office *after* the Black Sox Scandal. In fact, it was the Black Sox Scandal that prompted baseball to appoint a commissioner to keep the game free of gambling.

"And they say *Ah'm* dumb," Joe muttered.

"You could tell Commy," Katie suggested. I remembered that Commy was Charles Comiskey, the owner of the White Sox.

"Commy's a crook," chirped the bird. "Cheap Commy."

"Commy ain't gonna do nothin'," Joe said, hanging his head.

"You have to *try*, Joe!" Katie urged. She stuffed the money back into the envelope and stuffed the envelope into Joe's hand. Then she opened the door and gave him a shove. "Go! Tell him where you got this money!"

"Can I come?" I asked.

"Take the boy with you," Katie told Joe. "I need to go to sleep."

Reluctantly, Joe took the envelope and put it in the pocket of his bathrobe. He tightened the robe around himself and we left the room.

The Sinton Hotel must have been pretty big, because Joe led me up four flights of stairs and down a hallway that must have had at least twenty rooms. The hallways were empty except for us. A few dim lightbulbs lit the way. It occurred to me that fluorescent bulbs probably didn't exist yet.

"What room is your ma and pa stayin' in, Stosh?" Joe asked me.

"My ma and pa aren't here."

"Well, where are they?"

"In Louisville."

"You mean to say you came all the way from Louisville by *yourself* to see the Series?"

"Yup."

"You got any money?"

"My mom gave me twenty dollars."

"That oughta hold you for a spell. Where were you plannin' on sleepin' tonight, Stosh?"

"I guess I didn't think about it," I admitted.

"Stosh, you are *dumb*. Every hotel in Cincinnati is full 'cause of the Series. People are sleepin' in the parks."

"So I'll sleep in a park."

"Nothin' doin'," Joe said. "The park ain't safe for

a kid your age. You'll stay in the room with Katie and me."

"Okay, if you say so."

Finally, Joe stopped at Room 703 and knocked lightly at the door. There was no answer.

"Ah guess Commy ain't in," he said, turning to leave.

"Maybe he's asleep," I advised. "I think you have to knock harder."

Joe gave the door a good rap and stood there awkwardly. After a few seconds we heard some rustling inside, and the door opened. An older, gray-haired man blinked his eyes in the light of the hallway. He was wearing flannel pajamas, and he had a big nose.

"Mr. Comiskey, sir—"

"Jackson, what are you doing up this late?" Comiskey snapped, like a teacher scolding a kid he caught playing hookey. "You should be getting your rest for tomorrow. I'm counting on your bat to beat the Reds. And who's this kid?"

"My nephew, sir. There's somethin' you oughta know, Mr. Comiskey," Joe tried to explain. "The Series ain't on the square. Some of the boys sold out."

"That's the most ridiculous thing I've ever heard!" Comiskey thundered. "My boys would never sell me out. You woke me up to tell me *this* nonsense?"

"But, sir, Chick gave me this envelope. Look, it's stuffed with money."

"I don't care if it's stuffed with macaroni! Go to bed, Jackson. And send that kid home."

"What should Ah do with the money, sir?"

"Buy yourself some brains!"

Then he slammed the door in Joe's face.

# 14

# Scrap Paper

WHEN JOE AND I GOT BACK TO HIS HOTEL ROOM, KATIE was already asleep. The room was dark, and I couldn't see a thing. Joe pulled some matches out of his bathrobe pocket and lit a candle. He placed it on the dresser. Then he pulled a chair over so it was about four feet from the candle. He sat on the chair and stared at the flickering flame in silence.

I wasn't sure what to do. Joe was sort of an unusual guy. Maybe this was some kind of religious ceremony to him. For all I knew, maybe he slept sitting in a chair. Maybe he had trouble sleeping, and staring at a candle helped him nod off. I was feeling pretty tired myself, but I didn't think that crawling into the bed next to Joe's wife would be the right thing to do.

"What are you doing, Joe?" I finally whispered when my curiosity got the better of me.

"What's it look like?" he replied. "Ah'm lookin' at this candle. Sheesh, are you dumb about some stuff!"

"I mean *why* are you looking at the candle?"

"It sharpens my battin' eye," he said, covering one eye with his hand. "Half an hour every night. Fifteen minutes with one eye and fifteen minutes with the other."

I couldn't argue with the guy. His lifetime batting average was .356. One year he hit .408. Maybe *all* ballplayers should hold bats up in the air for a half an hour and stare at candles.

"Where do you want me to sleep, Joe?"

"There oughta be some blankets and pillows in the dresser drawer," he said, without moving his gaze away from the candle. "You can spread 'em out on the floor next to the bed."

I did as he said, making a little bed for myself. I took off my clothes except for my underwear and hung them carefully on the chair. I would have to wear them the next day. Then I went into the bathroom to pee and brush my teeth.

I hadn't thought to bring my toothbrush with me, so I just squeezed some of Joe and Katie's toothpaste onto my finger and rubbed my teeth the best that I could. Instead of Crest or Colgate, they had some stuff called Dr. Sheffield's Creme Dentifrice. It tasted awful.

When I came out of the bathroom, Joe was still staring at the candle. I slipped into my homemade bed. Even though I was tired, I didn't want to go to sleep yet. I couldn't get past the fact that I was with the great Shoeless Joe Jackson the night before the first game of the 1919 World Series.

"Is it okay to talk to you while you do that?" I whispered, trying not to wake Katie.

"It don't bother me none."

"What are you going to do tomorrow night?"

"Ah dunno," Joe replied. "You wanna go see a movie or somethin'?"

"Isn't the first game of the World Series tomorrow night?"

Joe shook his head, almost losing his gaze on the candle.

"And they say *Ah'm* dumb." He snorted. "How could we see the ball if we played at night? Don't you know nothin'?"

I smacked my head with my hand. How could I be so stupid? There were no night games in 1919!

"What I meant was, what are you going to do in the game tomorrow?" I corrected myself.

"Only thing Ah can do—try my durndest. Ah'll win it by myself if Ah have to."

I lay back on my pillow thinking things over. Watching *Eight Men Out* and talking to Flip Valentini had led me to believe Shoeless Joe Jackson had willingly taken the money from the gamblers. Now I knew that was wrong. He didn't ask for any money to throw the World Series, and he turned it down when it was offered to him. When the money was literally thrown at him, he tried to give it to the owner of the White Sox and tell him what was going on.

Shoeless Joe had done all he could. If the Black Sox Scandal was going to be stopped, I would have to stop it myself the next morning.

"Can I ask you a personal question, Joe?"

"Shoot," he replied, still staring intently at the candle.

"Why didn't you learn how to read?"

Joe's left hand clenched into a fist.

"There were eight kids in my family," he said softly. "Six boys and two girls. Ah was the oldest. My daddy didn't have no money. He worked in a cotton mill. He needed my help. Ah was workin' in the mill when Ah was eight years old. There was no time for school. None a my family never had schoolin'."

"But you could learn *now*," I suggested.

"Ah play ball," he stated simply. "It don't take no book learnin' or school stuff to help a fellow play ball. Don't need to read to hit the curve. Don't need to write to throw a guy out at the plate or catch a line drive. Ah make more money playin' ball than a whole lotta folks who can read 'n' write."

"What about after your baseball career is over?"

Joe quickly turned away from the candle and looked at me. There was a trace of anger in his eyes.

"Look, Ah'm only thirty," he said. "Ah got ten good years left if Ah stay healthy. Ah got a long way to go."

I knew something about him that Joe didn't.

Within a year, he would be thrown out of professional baseball for the rest of his life. His career would be over very soon. I knew he didn't want to hear that.

"But if you learned to read and write—"

"You think Ah *like* havin' everybody think Ah'm stupid?" he snapped. "You think Ah don't notice when Chick told Katie that maybe Ah don't know how much money twenty grand is 'cause Ah'm too dumb? You think Ah don't know Commy wouldn't listen to me 'cause he thinks Ah'm dumb? You think Ah don't hear the stuff people shout from the stands? You think Ah like bein' humiliated? Ah *hate* it."

"I'm sorry," I said. "I was only trying to help."

"Ah tried to learn," Joe said, more quietly. He hung his head a little. "Katie tried to teach me. Ah just couldn't do it. Here, look at this."

I crawled out of my homemade bed and went to where Joe was sitting. He opened the drawer and took out a fountain pen and some sheets of paper. All of the sheets were blank except for one. The one that wasn't blank looked like this:

BEST REGARDS
JOE JACKSON

My eyes opened wide. It looked *exactly* like the signature Flip Valentini had shown me in his book of famous autographs. Block letters. All capitals. The *A* was the same. The loop in the *J* was the same. I remembered that Flip had told me Joe Jackson's signature was one of the rarest in the world and that it was worth a half million dollars.

I held my breath as Joe picked up the pen awkwardly and began to write on a blank sheet of paper. He copied the letters slowly and carefully, sticking his tongue out as he labored over the paper. I could have written the words in a few seconds, but it took Joe at least ten minutes. He looked like an artist working on a painting.

When he was finished, he held the paper closer to the candle so he could see it better.

"Awful," he muttered, taking the sheet and sticking the corner of it into the flame.

"Don't burn it up!" I shouted, pushing his hand away from the candle. The tip of the page was charred, but it didn't ignite. Katie rolled over in the bed behind us but didn't wake up.

"Why not?" Joe asked, surprised.

"You'll set off the smoke detectors," I explained.

"The *what*?"

Oops! I had made another dumb mistake. There were no smoke detectors in 1919. Buildings used to burn down all the time back then.

"You might start a fire," I explained.

Joe shook his head, as if to say I was nuts. He

dropped the piece of paper into the little trash can next to the desk. As it fluttered into the basket all I could think of was that he had just thrown away a half million dollars. I tried not to react.

"That didn't look so bad," I said, encouragingly. "Try it again."

Joe took another sheet of paper and started over. Again, he painstakingly copied the autograph letter by letter. He didn't like that one very much either and tossed it in the trash.

I was counting in my head. That was one million dollars sitting in the garbage. I felt my heart racing in my chest.

"You're doing great," I said gently. "Why don't you try another one?"

Joe got as far as the word "best." When he messed up the $T$, he crumpled up the piece of paper in disgust and threw it away.

"Oh, heck, Ah just ain't no good at this stuff, and that's all there is to it. Everything they write about me in the newspapers is lies anyway, so what's the point in learnin' how to read or write?"

Joe blew out the candle and climbed into bed next to his sleeping wife. I slipped into my bed on the floor.

"Good night, Joe."

"G'night, Stosh."

I lay there for a long time thinking. Not more than five feet away from me there was a wastebasket with the equivalent of a million dollars in it!

I could buy a lot of stuff with a million dollars. A new house and car for my mom. A motorcycle for my dad. He's always wanted one. And for me, well, I could pretty much clean out a sporting goods store.

Should I take the autographs out of the garbage? I lay there thinking. Those autographs didn't belong to me. They didn't belong to *anybody*. They were garbage. Joe Jackson didn't offer them to me. He threw them away. His *intention* was to burn them. Maybe it would be wrong for me to take them.

Or maybe it would be right. I mean, who would it hurt if I kept a couple of pieces of paper that were in the garbage? Nobody. Technically, I wouldn't be stealing anything. It would be more like scavenging or picking up a penny somebody had dropped in the street. I could always get Joe's permission in the morning. Besides, I told myself, he never told me that I *couldn't* have the signatures.

It seemed so long ago that I had been hired to clean out the attic of Amanda Young, the old lady who used to live next door to me. That was where I found the valuable Honus Wagner card I had used to take my first trip through time. Back then, I thought long and hard about whether the right thing to do was for me to keep the card for myself or give it back to Miss Young. In the end, I decided to give it back to her.

Once again, I had a decision to make. I lay there for a long time trying to decide what was the right thing to do.

Joe's breathing got slower, and in a few minutes he began to snore. Joe and Katie were asleep.

I crept on my hands and knees in the dark until I was able to find the trash can. I picked out the two scraps of paper and put them inside the pocket of my pants.

# 15

## Wake-up Call

THE FIRST THING I NOTICED WHEN I WOKE UP IN THE morning was that my nose wasn't running anymore. I was going to take one of my flu pills, but decided not to. I was all better.

The second thing I noticed was the sound of the telephone ringing. I looked at Joe and Katie's bed. It was empty. The shower was running in the bathroom, so I figured one or both of them were in there. I picked up the phone.

"This is your wake-up call," a gruff voice barked before I could even say hello.

"Huh?" I asked, glancing at the clock on the night table. It was nine o'clock.

"Where's Jackson?" the voice on the phone asked.

It occurred to me that this might be one of the gamblers who had locked me in the closet.

"Jackson's not here," I said, trying to disguise my voice.

"Who are you?"

"I'm his nephew," I lied. "Who is this?"

"Never mind who I am," the guy said. "You just tell your uncle Joe to make sure everything goes according to the plan today. Or else."

"Or else what?" I asked.

Click. The guy had hung up.

I had a pretty good idea of what he meant, and I didn't like it. The guy must be some gambler putting his money on the Cincinnati Reds to win. "The plan today" had to be that the White Sox were going to lose the first game of the World Series. If they won, the guy on the phone was going to lose money. And if he lost money, he was going to do something bad to Joe. That's what "or else" had to mean.

I put the phone down, disturbed. But my mood brightened considerably when the bathroom door opened and Katie walked through it. She was drying her hair with a towel. Otherwise, she had nothing on. I realized that I was still in my underwear.

"Eeeeeeeeeeeeeeeeeeeeeeeeeek!"

Katie hastily wrapped the towel around herself.

"What are *you* still doing here?" she asked.

"I'm sorry!" I said, feeling my face flush with embarrassment. I started pulling on my clothes. "Didn't Joe tell you? He said it was okay for me to stay over last night. I slept on the floor on the other side of the bed. I guess you didn't notice me."

"How come you always seem to be around when I'm naked?" Katie asked, somewhat amused.

"Just lucky, I guess," I replied. "Where's Joe?"

Katie looked around the room.

"Black Betsy isn't here. Joe probably walked over to Redland Park. He likes to get to the ballpark early for batting practice."

"I've got to talk with him," I said, tucking my shirt in. I rushed out the door before she could ask me why.

The doorman in the hotel lobby told me how to get to Redland Park. It was less than a mile from the Sinton Hotel. The street was already clogged with people, and cars belching smoke. There was a sense of excitement in the air. I glanced at a newspaper a guy was selling on the corner.

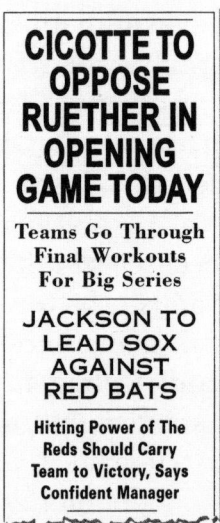

**CICOTTE TO OPPOSE RUETHER IN OPENING GAME TODAY**

Teams Go Through Final Workouts For Big Series

**JACKSON TO LEAD SOX AGAINST RED BATS**

Hitting Power of The Reds Should Carry Team to Victory, Says Confident Manager

About five blocks from the hotel, there was a park. Just like Joe had said, people were camped out there. Some of them were cooking breakfast over little stoves. Others were still sleeping.

At one corner of the park was a baseball diamond. A bunch of boys around my age were tossing a ball back and forth. I went a little closer to get a better look.

That's when I saw Joe.

He was in his street clothes, playing "pepper" with the boys. I had heard of the game, but I'd never played it. In my time, nobody played pepper.

Joe had Black Betsy in his hand, and six or seven boys were lined up about ten yards away from him. A boy would flip a ball to Joe, and he would slap a one-hopper back at the line of boys. Whichever one fielded the one-hopper would toss it back to Joe, who would slap it again. Only a few of the boys were wearing mitts, but they were pretty good fielders anyway.

With a bat in his hand, Joe had a relaxed, easy manner. He was graceful, like a big cat. Joe had incredible bat control. He was able to place the ball precisely where he wanted it. If a boy called out, "Me next, Mr. Jackson," Joe would hit it right to that kid.

I looked at Joe's face as he played with the boys. He had this sweet smile that I hadn't seen up until this point. He looked like a little boy himself. He seemed so incredibly happy.

"How about a show out, Mr. Jackson!" one of the boys hollered.

"Yeah, do a show out, Joe!"

I had no idea what a show out was. It must be

some word from long ago, I figured.

"You boys don't want to see me hurt my arm before the World Series, do you?" Joe asked.

"Just one?" a young boy pleaded.

"Well, okay," Joe said. "Catcher's keepers."

The boys dashed away and spread themselves out across the deep outfield. Joe took the ball in his hand and gripped it carefully. Then he took a couple of hopping steps forward from home plate, wound up, and let it fly.

I had seen home-run hitting contests on TV back home, but I had never seen anything like *this*. The ball took off like a missile, soaring far over the heads of all the boys. It looked like it would never come down. It sailed right out of the park. The boys went dashing off after the ball. Joe laughed himself silly.

It seemed like a good time to speak to him, so I ran over.

"Joe!" I hollered.

"Stosh! You eat yet?"

There was a little coffee shop on the next corner, and Joe steered me inside. We took seats on stools at the counter. The waitress didn't recognize him. She handed us each a menu and stood there. Joe picked his up and looked it over carefully. I watched him, knowing full well he didn't know how to read. I realized that he was pretending to read the menu for the benefit of the waitress.

"Ah'll have the ham and eggs," he finally said, handing back the menu.

"Me too," I said.

"Sleep okay, Stosh?"

"Yeah. Your wife was kind of surprised to see me in your room."

"Ah forgot to tell her," Joe admitted sheepishly.

A guy sitting next to us was smoking a cigarette. I looked around to see if we could move to the nonsmoking section. That's when I realized that in 1919, there was no such thing as a nonsmoking section.

Joe and I made some small talk, and soon the ham and eggs arrived. He gobbled his up and washed them down with a cup of coffee. Finally I worked up the nerve to tell him about the "wake-up call" I'd taken for him.

"Tell me again what the guy said?" Joe asked, his forehead wrinkled with worry.

"He told me to tell you to make sure that everything goes according to the plan today," I recited. "Or else."

Joe thought about the words, then the expression on his face changed. The boyish look of happiness he'd had a few minutes earlier was completely gone. The look of worry was gone, too. It was replaced with a look of fierce determination.

He slapped a dollar bill on the counter and got up from his stool.

"Let's go to the ballpark. Ah got me a game to win."

# 16

# The World Series

AS JOE AND I GOT CLOSER TO REDLAND PARK, THE streets became clogged with people. The color red was everywhere. Women were wearing red dresses. Men had on red shirts. There were red flags, pennants, and banners. I was struck by all the bright color. All the old-time photos I had seen were black and white, so I assumed the whole world must have *been* black and white back in those days.

Joe pulled his hat low over his eyes so he wouldn't be pestered for autographs.

It was a good day to play baseball. The skies were blue and clear. It felt like 80 degrees or so. Some men had taken off their jackets but not their hats. It was like the hats were surgically attached to their heads. I wondered if they *slept* with their hats on.

When we reached Redland Park, a marching band—dressed in red uniforms, of course—was standing in the street playing "Hail, Hail, the Gang's All Here." The overpoweringly wonderful smell of roasted peanuts wafted past.

The whole atmosphere looked like one big street party. It occurred to me that in 1919 "the national pastime" wasn't just a nickname for baseball. Baseball really *was* the national game. There was no NBA or NFL in 1919. Baseball was the only spectator sport around.

Near the ticket booths, six men wearing army uniforms were standing in a group, drinking whiskey. It took me a moment to realize what was unusual about them—three of them had only one leg. They must have been injured in World War I and had a leg amputated.

Still, the soldiers seemed happy. *Everyone* seemed happier than usual. I wondered if people were simply happier back in 1919.

Then it occurred to me that these people were survivors. They had survived the war. They had survived the influenza epidemic that killed millions of people. And their hometown team—the Reds— had made it to the World Series for the first time. No wonder they were happy.

Everyone, it seemed, was holding a bottle in their hand. A lot of them looked like they were already drunk. I'd seen grown-ups drinking before, but never like this. I mentioned it to Joe.

"Let 'em drink while they can," he mumbled. "The Eighteenth Amendment becomes law in January."

"The Eighteenth Amendment? What's that?"

Joe looked at me again like I was stupid and shook his head in wonder. "Ain'tcha heard about Prohibition? They're makin' all booze illegal. Three months from now, they won't be able to buy themselves a drink."

I remembered learning something about Prohibition in school, but I didn't remember when it took place.

Joe hustled me past some drunks milling around the ticket booth. Box seats were selling for $1.10, and bleacher seats for just fifty cents.

"Get your World Series program!" a vendor hollered. "Twenty-five cents!"

I thought about buying one. It would be a cool souvenir to bring home. But Joe seemed to be in a hurry. He had his hand on my shoulder and steered me into a side entrance marked VISITORS.

"Are you going to tell your teammates I'm your nephew?" I asked.

"Don't need to tell 'em nothin'."

We made our way to the locker room, and it was nothing like I had expected. There was no music, no laughter, no card games. The players were like two rival gangs, with one group on one side of the room and the other group on the other side. They mumbled in low tones as they put their uniforms on and shot glances across the room. I wondered if the players who weren't involved in the fix even knew it was going on.

I recognized Chick Gandil, who had come to Joe's

hotel room the night before. I couldn't tell who the other players were, because they didn't have names or numbers on their uniforms. I guessed that must

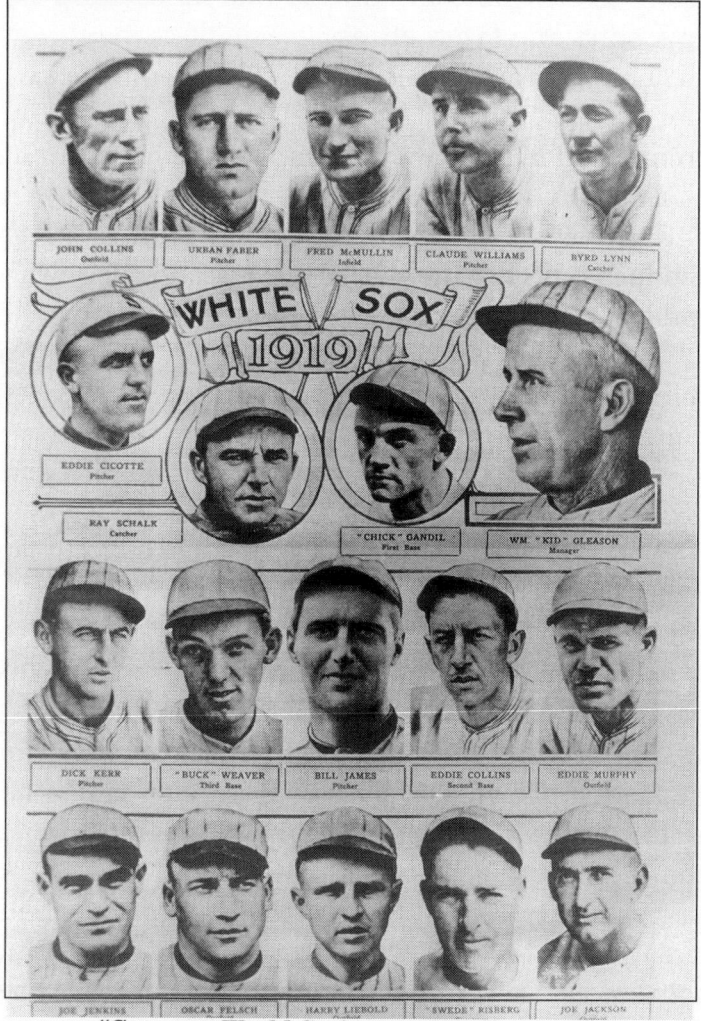

"Get your World Series program!" a vendor hollered. "Twenty-five cents!"

have come after 1919, and I was relieved that I hadn't done something stupid like ask Joe his number.

"What's a kid doin' in here?" a big guy said to Joe when he saw us come in. He was dressed up in a pink shirt and fancy shoes.

"Leave the kid be, Eddie," Joe replied curtly, then he threw me a wink. "He's my nephew, from Louisville."

*Eddie must be Eddie Cicotte*, I thought to myself. The pitcher. He was the guy who called on the phone last night and offered Joe money to throw the game.

"How come you ain't never told us about no nephew from Louisville?" Cicotte asked suspiciously.

"Ah don't tell you everythin', Eddie," Joe said, turning away from him.

Nobody else seemed to care that I was there. Joe went to his locker and put on his uniform, a pin-striped, dirty old thing that hung off him as if it was a few sizes too large. The word "Sox" was written with one big $S$, and the $O$ and $X$ sat in the curves of the $S$. There was an American flag on the left sleeve. Joe pulled on his cap, which had a much smaller brim than my baseball caps at home.

Somebody said it was time to shoot the team picture, and the players lumbered through the clubhouse door and into the dugout, their spikes clattering against the concrete floor. I followed.

The field was big—bigger than our fields.

Centerfield looked like it was a mile away. There were billboards on the outfield walls—Pepsi-Cola, Cracker Jack, Ever-Ready Safety Razor. In the apartment buildings beyond the outfield wall, I could see binoculars popping out of every window. People were also up on the roofs and hanging on to telephone poles.

While Joe looked out on the field, I pulled out my little camera and snapped his picture. He didn't seem to notice.

A photographer with an enormous camera on a tripod gathered the players around. I told Joe that he'd missed two buttons on his shirt, and he buttoned them. Then he took a spot right in the back row, throwing his arm around the player next to him. I stood off to the side and a little behind the photographer.

**While Joe looked out on the field, I pulled out my little camera and snapped his picture. He didn't seem to notice.**

Looking at the White Sox, I thought they appeared to be the most serious, unfriendly group of men I had ever seen.

"Come on, boys," the photographer hollered. "Show some teeth! You're gonna be World Champions!"

"Don't bet on it," Chick Gandil cracked.

When the players laughed, the photographer tripped the shutter. I took a picture, too.

A roar erupted from the crowd, and I turned around to see the Cincinnati Reds jog out of their dugout. They were wearing white uniforms with red trim and piping. On their uniform front was a big *C* curled around the word "Reds." Naturally, they wore red stockings.

**When the players laughed, the photographer tripped the shutter. I took a picture, too.**

I took a seat in the Chicago dugout near a short, older guy while the players played catch with each other. The ballpark was beginning to fill up. The bleachers in right field, I noticed, were just wooden planks. Fans out there were blowing horns and clanging bells. Red, white, and blue flags were draped over the more expensive seats on the first and third baselines, where the rich people sat.

The scoreboard wasn't electronic. I could see somebody sitting inside it, fiddling with big wooden numbers he would put up when runs were scored.

The other thing that caught my eye was the gloves the players were using. They were much smaller than the one I used in Little League, and the fingers were not even connected with laces. The ball had to be caught right in the palm of the hand.

While I was looking around, Shoeless Joe had jogged over and approached the short guy who had been pacing up and down the Sox dugout.

"Skip," Joe moaned, "Ah don't feel too good."

"What's the matter, Jackson?" the guy replied. I assumed he was the White Sox manager.

"Ah dunno. Ah'm sick, Ah reckon. Maybe you better bench me."

"Nothing doing," he told Joe. "I need Black Betsy in the lineup. It's just nerves. Shake it off, Joe. You can take a good long rest after we whip these bushers."

Joe hung his head and walked away. He grabbed a bunch of bats and sat down on the dirt outside the dugout. Using a cloth and some kind of oil, he lovingly rubbed each bat.

"This here's Blonde Betsy," he explained when he saw the puzzled look on my face. "And this is Caroliny."

"Do you name all your bats?" I asked.

"Well, sure! There's Ol' Genril over here and this one's Big Jim. You boys gonna get me some hits today?"

A fan with a Cincinnati pennant leaned over the fence and yelled to Joe, "Hey, professor! You read any good books lately?"

**He grabbed a bunch of bats and sat down on the dirt
outside the dugout. Using a cloth and some kind of oil,
he lovingly rubbed each bat.**

Joe just spit in the guy's direction. He picked up Black Betsy and walked up to the plate for batting practice. He ripped the first three pitches over the rightfield wall. Then he looked over at the Cincinnati fan who had yelled at him. The guy's mouth hung open. Some of the guys on the Reds looked on in awe, too.

It was almost two o'clock, according to the scoreboard. The players cleared the field, and the managers came out to give their lineup cards to the umpire. A marching band came out to home plate. The crowd got to its feet as "The Star-Spangled Banner" was played.

The umpire picked up a huge megaphone, which I guessed was the only public address system they had in 1919. He was about to say something when a loud noise was heard in the distance. It sounded like a lawn mower to me.

Everybody stopped what they were doing and looked up in the sky. It was a little airplane, one of those old-fashioned ones where each side has two wings, one on top of the other. People in the stands pointed and gazed with wonder as the plane circled the field.

I remembered reading that the one hundredth anniversary of the first flight was in 2003. That meant the Wright Brothers got off the ground in 1903. So the airplane was only sixteen years old in 1919. No wonder all the people were looking up. Not only had they never *been* in a plane, but many of them probably had never *seen* one before.

The plane made a few lazy circles over Redland Park. Then I saw something drop out of it. As the thing plummeted to the ground, I could see arms and legs flopping around. It was a person!

The crowd gasped. Some women shrieked. The body slammed into the pitcher's mound with a dull thud and lay there motionless. The plane flew away.

A policeman rushed out on the field. He bent over the body for a few seconds, then scooped it up in his arms. The cop had a big smile on his face.

The thing that was thrown from the plane was a dummy . . . wearing a Chicago White Sox uniform.

There was nervous laughter in the stands, and then the umpire picked up the megaphone again.

"Play ball!" he hollered.

# 17

# The Fix Is On

THE FIRST THING THE WHITE SOX DID WAS TO KICK ME out of the dugout. The fact that I was supposedly Joe Jackson's nephew did not carry much weight with the players.

"No kids on the bench!" Chick Gandil announced.

Shoeless Joe shrugged and said I should stop by after the game. I slinked out through the clubhouse door and into the stands. Because I didn't have a ticket, I wandered around looking for an empty seat. There weren't any. Redland Park was packed.

Down on the field, a guy with a megaphone announced that Dutch Ruether would be the pitcher for the Reds. He was a lefty. The Cincinnati crowd gave him a big round of applause. Shano Collins, the leadoff guy for the Sox, stepped up to the plate. I hadn't heard of him, and I didn't think he was in on the fix.

"I got fifty cents that says Collins gets a hit," a guy near me yelled as a fastball zipped outside for ball one.

"Betcha buck he strikes out!" replied somebody else.

"You're on, buddy."

Bets were flying back and forth among the fans like Ping-Pong balls. I'd never heard anything like it before. Many of the spectators sounded like they hadn't come to watch the game; they only came to place bets on it.

The next pitch was high for ball two, and then Collins took a called strike. Even without a megaphone, the umpire's voice could be heard throughout the ballpark.

With the count at 2-1, Collins ripped a single up the middle. The Reds fans moaned, and some money changed hands in the stands.

The next hitter for the Sox was also named Collins—Eddie Collins. A left-handed batter. He took a wad of gum out of his mouth and stuck it on the button of his cap as he stepped into the batter's box. Collins took a couple of pitches, then dropped down a bunt. The pitcher grabbed it and whipped it to second for the force play. One out.

Collins edged off first as Buck Weaver came up. Shoeless Joe, with Black Betsy in his hands, came out on deck. On the first pitch to Weaver, Collins broke for second base, but the Cincinnati catcher made a perfect throw and nailed him. Two outs.

Weaver lifted a fly ball to left center for the third

out. Disgustedly, Shoeless Joe put Betsy away and jogged out to his position in leftfield. He would have to wait until the second inning for a chance to hit.

I watched as Eddie Cicotte walked slowly to the mound. I wondered what he was thinking. The megaphone man announced that Cicotte had led the American League in wins with 29, complete games with 30, and innings pitched with 307. He was one of the best pitchers in the game.

But he had been paid to *lose*. Would he just lob the ball up to the plate and let the Reds hammer it? Would he miss the plate on purpose and walk everybody? Or would he wait for the perfect moment with the bases loaded and throw one fat pitch that would cost the Sox the game?

**I watched as Eddie Cicotte walked slowly to the mound. I wondered what he was thinking.**

I remembered that Rothstein had instructed that the first batter for the Reds was to be hit by a pitch as a signal that the Sox were doing as they had been told.

The leadoff hitter for the Reds—a guy named Maurice Rath—stepped up to the plate. Cicotte rubbed the baseball against his pants leg.

"Shiner," a guy near me commented. "He's throwing his shine ball."

I didn't know what a shine ball was, but I remembered from my baseball history that starting in 1920 it became illegal for pitchers to throw spitballs, scuffballs, and other tricky pitches. In 1919, Cicotte could do pretty much whatever he wanted to the ball.

The first pitch was up around the chest, but the ump called it a strike. Maybe Cicotte had changed his mind and decided to play straight. Maybe the fix wasn't on after all.

Cicotte went into his windup again, but this time the pitch was way inside. Rath dove out of the way, but the ball smacked him right between the shoulder blades.

That was the signal. The fix was on. Cicotte was playing to lose, and so were most of the other White Sox starters. It would be up to Joe Jackson and the other honest players to win the game in spite of them.

Rath got up slowly and jogged to first base. The next batter, Jake Daubert, smacked a single up the middle. The Reds had runners on first and third with nobody out. The Cincinnati crowd was screaming for a hit. It looked like Eddie Cicotte was going to blow the whole game right there in the first inning.

But he didn't. The next Cincinnati batter was Heinie Groh, the guy whose baseball card got me to 1919 in the first place. Groh had a weird bat that was shaped almost like a bottle. He hit a shot to leftfield. Shoeless Joe ran back almost to the fence to make a great catch. The runner on third tagged up on the play and scored.

The next two Reds were retired easily on grounders. I thought Chick Gandil, the first baseman, might drop the ball on purpose, but he didn't. The Sox were out of the inning and the score was 1-0. It could have been a lot worse.

**I thought Chick Gandil, the first baseman, might drop the ball on purpose, but he didn't. The Sox were out of the inning and the score was 1-0.**

When Joe Jackson came out of the dugout to lead off the second inning, a hush fell over the crowd. They knew that if Jackson got hot, he could carry the White Sox on his shoulders.

"Give 'em Black Betsy, Joe!" a Chicago fan shouted as Joe approached the plate.

Using his toe, Joe drew a line in the dirt about three inches from home plate on the left-hander's side. Then he made a right angle at the back of the batter's box and carefully put his left foot on it. His feet were close together. He rested the bat on his left shoulder, holding the bat at the end so his right pinky curled around the knob.

Ruether went into his windup and pumped strike one over. Joe just looked at it. He didn't wave the bat around like some of the other players. He just stood there, motionless. He watched as ball one came in too low.

**He rested the bat on his left shoulder, holding the bat at the end so his right pinky curled around the knob.**

The next pitch he liked. Joe took a long stride and smashed a hot grounder in the hole at short. The Cincinnati shortstop dove for it and knocked the ball down, but his throw to first was wild. Joe never stopped running and slid into second base in a cloud of dust and dirt.

The few Chicago fans, who were sitting as a group on the third-base side, cheered happily. It looked like it could be a big inning for the Sox.

The next batter, Happy Felsch, bunted to advance Joe to third base. Chick Gandil was up next. I figured he'd strike out on purpose, but he hit a high fly to short leftfield. None of the Reds could reach it, and Shoeless Joe trotted home for the first Chicago run. The other Sox went down quietly, but the game was tied at 1-1.

The Reds went down one-two-three in the bottom of the second, and nobody scored in the third inning. Once again, I was beginning to hope and believe that maybe the game was being played on the level. Maybe something had happened. Some of the Sox might have changed their minds, come to their senses, and decided to play their best.

But then came the fourth inning, when Eddie Cicotte and the White Sox collapsed. With one out, Pat Duncan singled to right center. The next batter hit a bouncer right back to Cicotte. Easy double-play ball that would end the inning. But Cicotte hesitated before throwing, and then made a low throw to second. The runner was out there, but there was no chance for the double play.

That's when Cicotte collapsed. Greasy Neale singled up the middle. Ivey Wingo singled to right on the first pitch to drive in a run. Dutch Ruether—the pitcher!—whacked a triple for two more runs. That made it 4-1 and the crowd was going crazy.

I saw somebody start warming up in the Sox bullpen. The infielders gathered at the mound to try and calm down Eddie Cicotte.

Whatever they said had no effect. Maurice Rath ripped a double down the third baseline to drive in another run. Jake Daubert singled to right to make it 6-1.

That made it six hits and five runs scored in one inning. The Chicago fans on the third-base side had sunk into a silent gloom. The Sox manager marched angrily out of the dugout and waved to the bullpen for a relief pitcher to come in. As Eddie Cicotte walked off the mound, the Cincinnati fans hooted and threw fruit at him. Cicotte hung his head all the way to the dugout.

The new pitcher stopped the hitting spree, but the damage was done. The Sox looked terrible. There was nothing Shoeless Joe could do, and there was nothing I could do that would change the outcome of this game. I didn't even feel like watching the rest of it.

I looked up at the scoreboard. It was the end of the fourth inning. Suddenly I remembered that I had made a mental note to do a chore at the end of the fourth inning. It had nothing to do with baseball.

I had to go find Gladys and Wilbur Kozinsky.

# 18

# The Meeting

AS I MADE MY WAY TO THE THIRD-BASE SIDE OF THE stands at Redland Park, I began to look for my great-grandmother Gladys Kozinsky and her brother Wilbur. Not that I really wanted to see them or anything, but my mother had asked me to take their picture. Sometimes you've got to do stuff just for your mom whether you like it or not.

The Cincinnati fans I walked past looked like a bunch of kids on Christmas morning. Their Reds were killing the Sox, and the fans were loving it. People were hugging each other, laughing, throwing stuff. If they had known the Sox were blowing the game on purpose, I doubt that they would have been celebrating so enthusiastically.

Gladys and Wilbur shouldn't be hard to spot, I figured. After all, they were twins. My mom had told me they were twelve years old in 1919. And Gladys told me to meet them at the hot dog vendor on the third-base side.

There were a few boys and girls near the hot dog vendor, but none of them looked like twins. Watching them eat made me a little hungry, so I got in line.

"What'll it be, son?" the hot dog guy asked when it was my turn.

"One hot dog, please," I said, fishing around in my pocket for the twenty-dollar bill my mom had given me.

"That'll be five cents, sonny."

"Five cents?!"

Five cents for a hot dog? The last time I went to a ballpark, my dad had to pay three dollars for a hot dog.

"Whatsa matter?" the hot dog guy asked, as I was still hunting for the bill in my pocket. "You ain't got a nickel?"

"All I have is a twenty-dollar bill."

"Ain'tcha got nothin' smaller?" the hot dog guy asked, looking at me with disgust. "Sonny, I don't make that much dough all *week*."

I stuck my hands in my pockets, but all I could find was my medicine, my camera, and my baseball cards.

"Rich kids," the hot dog guy grumbled under his breath.

"I'll pay for his hot dog," somebody chirped behind me.

I turned around. It was a girl about my age, with long, kinky hair that was pulled back from her forehead. She held out a nickel to the hot dog guy and smiled at me.

The hot dog guy took the nickel and handed me the dog. I thanked the girl and took a bite. It tasted good.

"You have twenty dollars?" the girl asked, impressed.

"Somewhere in here," I replied. "My mom gave it to me."

"Your mama must be loaded, giving a boy your age so much money."

She flicked her eyelashes up and down, still smiling at me.

"Not really," I replied.

Twenty dollars, I gathered, must have been *big* money in 1919. My mother once told me we weren't rich and we weren't poor, but we were a lot closer to poor than rich. She also told me that if a girl ever flicks her eyelashes as you, it means she thinks you're cute. I tried not to blush.

"Let's *go*, Gladys!" urged a boy standing about ten feet away. "I got a headache!" The boy was wearing a white mask that covered his nose and mouth, the kind of mask doctors wear on TV when they do surgery. He had a book in his hand titled *Captain Billy's Whiz Bang*.

"Shut up, Wilbur," the girl replied. Then she whispered to him, "He's *rich*!"

"*You* shut up," the boy responded.

*Gladys? Wilbur?* Suddenly I realized the boy and

girl were my great-grandmother and her brother!

"Are you Gladys Kozinsky?" I asked, marveling that this girl in front of me would grow up to be my great-grandmother.

"Why, yes!" She smiled, holding out a hand. "And who might you be?"

"Joe. Joe Stoshack."

Gladys looked puzzled. "The boy who called me on the telephone? I was looking for somebody with a camera. How are you going to snap our picture if you don't have a camera?"

"With this," I said, pulling the Olympus out of my pocket.

"You're going to take a photo with that little bitty thing?" She giggled uncontrollably. "Look, Wilbur. It's a toy!"

I wasn't about to explain to them how computer chips had made it possible for many machines to be much smaller than they used to be. They probably didn't even know what a computer was.

Wilbur didn't seem interested anyway. He stood off to the side, tapping his foot impatiently, reading his book, and smoking a cigarette. Whenever he took a puff, he pulled the surgical mask away from his mouth.

I wondered if wearing a mask was some weird 1919 fad. A number of fans were wearing them. I thought about telling Wilbur that smoking was bad for his health, but he looked like he might punch me or something.

"It's . . . a new camera," I said simply. "Hey, I

thought you were twins. You don't look anything like your brother."

It was true. Wilbur was more fair-skinned, with straighter hair and squinty eyes. It was hard to tell exactly what he looked like with that mask on his face, but he sure didn't look like Gladys.

"We're not identical," she said. "Do you still want to snap our picture?"

"Sure," I said, fiddling with the camera. I couldn't stop glancing at Wilbur's silly mask. It couldn't be a Halloween costume. It was only October 1.

"Why is your brother wearing that mask?" I whispered to Gladys when my curiosity got the better of me.

Gladys looked at me like I was stupid. She pointed to a sign that had been tacked up to a wooden post behind the hot dog guy.

"Wilbur's got the flu," she said.

I was going to say "Me, too," but stopped myself. The *flu*, I realized for the first time, was the same as *influenza*. I remembered the newspaper article I'd seen in the bathroom yesterday. It said millions of people died in the influenza epidemic of 1918, even more people than died in World War I.

"Shouldn't he be home?" I asked.

"He's not going to get better at home," she replied. "There's no cure."

"Is he going to die?" I whispered to Gladys.

"We don't know," she whispered back. "I hope not. He was fine yesterday. And then he got the fever . . ."

INFLUENZA
FREQUENTLY COMPLICATED WITH
PNEUMONIA
IS PREVALENT AT THIS TIME THROUGHOUT AMERICA.
THIS BALLPARK IS CO-OPERATING WITH THE DEPARTMENT OF HEALTH.
YOU MUST DO THE SAME
IF YOU HAVE A COLD AND ARE COUGHING AND
SNEEZING DO NOT ENTER THIS BALLPARK
GO HOME AND GO TO BED UNTIL YOU ARE WELL

Coughing, Sneezing or Spitting Will Not Be
Permitted In The Ballpark. In case you must
cough or Sneeze, do so in your own handkerchief and if the Coughing or Sneezing
Persists Leave The Ballpark At Once.

This Ballpark has agreed to co-operate with
the Department of Health in disseminating
the truth about Influenza and thus serve
a great educational purpose.

HELP US TO KEEP CINCINNATI THE
HEALTHIEST CITY IN THE WORLD
JOHN DILL ROBERTSON
COMMISSIONER OF HEALTH

**Gladys pointed to a sign that had been tacked up to a wooden post behind the hot dog guy.**

I didn't know what to say. Wilbur stood off to the side, smoking his cigarette. I noticed for the first time that he was hugging his arms around himself, as if he was trying to stay warm.

"So you wanna take my picture or not?" he snapped.

"Yeah, I do."

I stepped forward so I could frame him in the camera's viewfinder.

"Take off the mask, Wilbur," Gladys instructed her brother, "and smile pretty."

**Wilbur took the mask off his face and slipped it into his pocket. The picture looked pretty good through the viewfinder, so I pushed the button. Then I took one of Gladys.**

Wilbur took the mask off his face and slipped it into his pocket. He didn't exactly smile, but I guess he didn't have much to smile about. The picture looked pretty good through the viewfinder, so I pushed the button. Then I took one of Gladys.

"What kinda picture's that little thing gonna shoot?" Wilbur asked. "Postage stamps?"

"It takes thirty-five millimeter film," I explained. "You blow it up."

"Sounds dangerous!" Gladys exclaimed. "I'll leave blowing things up to you two boys. I've got to visit the powder room. Will you excuse me for a moment?"

Gladys sashayed off, leaving Wilbur and me

alone. I never was much for small talk, so I decided to keep my mouth shut rather than say something stupid. Wilbur put his mask back on and returned to reading *Captain Billy's Whiz Bang*.

There was a roar from the crowd. I glanced at the scoreboard. The Reds had scored two more runs. Now the score was 8-1. I thought about commenting on how well the Reds were playing, but Wilbur didn't seem to care about the game.

"Where'd you get them pants?" Wilbur suddenly asked as he took a puff from his cigarette.

The question took me by surprise. Boys my age don't usually talk about stuff like clothes. I looked down at my pants. They were the pants my mom had found in that box up in the—

Wait a minute! I looked at Wilbur's pants.

*They looked exactly like mine!*

Could Wilbur and I be wearing the *same* pair of pants at the same time? Would it actually be possible for somebody to save somebody's pants for eight decades, travel back through time wearing the pants, and then meet the guy whose pants you're wearing while he was wearing the same pants?

Or did Wilbur simply have a closet full of the same pants?

In any case, it was pretty cool.

"I guess we got them at the same store," I replied.

"Yeah, probably."

Suddenly, Wilbur started coughing violently. He

doubled over, hacking and wheezing. When he was finally able to get control of himself, he dropped the cigarette and stepped on it.

"Smoking is bad for you," I pointed out.

"It ain't the smoking," Wilbur replied, grinding the butt into the ground. "It's the flu."

I thought about taking another picture of Wilbur but decided against it. I slipped the camera back into my pocket. As I did, my fingers brushed against my medicine bottle. I stopped.

*The flu.*

I was just getting over the flu. Wilbur had just come down with it. We had the same thing! Maybe my medicine could help Wilbur. I pulled the plastic container from my pocket.

"Wilbur," I said urgently, "I want you to have this."

"Tamiflu," he said, reading the label. "What is it?"

"Medicine for the flu," I told him.

"There ain't no medicine for the flu," Wilbur said. "The doctor told me so. He said nothin' does any good."

"Just *take* it," I urged him. "It might make you feel better."

"Couldn't hurt," he said, slipping the container into his pocket.

Gladys flounced back from the bathroom, bouncing over to me with her flirty smile.

"Mr. Joe Stoshack," she bubbled, "I just had the

most marvelous idea! Why don't you come over to our house for dinner tonight? We can celebrate the Reds' victory. I'm sure Mother won't mind."

"Thanks anyway," I said, as her smile vanished instantly, "but I've got to be getting back home tonight."

"Well, maybe some other time then," she said, trying to hide her disappointment. "We'd love to see your little pictures."

"Yeah," I agreed. "Maybe some other time."

# 19

## Alert the Media

AS I WATCHED THE KOZINSKYS WALK BACK TO THEIR seats, there was a roar from the crowd. Dutch Ruether, the Cincinnati pitcher, had smashed a triple with a runner on base. The Reds had scored another run. That made it 9-1.

The game was essentially over. Many of the fans had left the ballpark. The World Series was over, as far as I was concerned. There was no point in going back to the Sox dugout. I sat in the nearest empty seat to watch the ninth inning.

Joe led off for the Sox. Desperately, I hoped he'd get a rally going. I knew there had been times when a team came back after being eight runs behind. Maybe a miracle would happen.

But it didn't. Joe flied out to left. Happy Felsch flied out, too. The last hope for the White Sox was Chick Gandil, who of course was in on the fix. He dribbled a weak grounder to second.

The game was over. I looked up at the score-board:

| | 1 | 2 | 3 | 4 | 5 | 6 | 7 | 8 | 9 |
|-----|---|---|---|---|---|---|---|---|---|
| **CHI** | 0 | 1 | 0 | 0 | 0 | 0 | 0 | 0 | 1 |
| **CIN** | 1 | 0 | 0 | 5 | 0 | 0 | 2 | 1 | - | 9 |

Pathetic. The best team in baseball had been crushed, humiliated. I sat there watching the happy Cincinnati fans make their way to the exits. Soon all that was left were crumpled candy wrappers, peanut shells, and discarded programs.

A wave of sadness came over me. My mission had been to prevent the Black Sox Scandal and save Shoeless Joe Jackson. I had failed at both jobs.

I was feeling sorry for myself but at the same time feeling that I had at least *tried* to do something good. What could I have expected, anyway? I was just a kid. Even if I was a grown-up, you can't change history. My science teacher said so himself. I should have known better.

A thought flashed through my mind. While I hadn't been able to prevent the Black Sox Scandal, *the scandal hadn't happened yet*! At this point, min-utes after Game 1, the world didn't know the Series had been fixed. The world wouldn't know about the scandal until the newspapers uncovered the story and printed it.

I turned around in my seat trying to find the press box, where the reporters sit during games and write their articles for the next day's paper. There was no press box. But at the other side of the field, I could see a line of about ten men sitting along the first baseline behind the dugout. I rushed over there.

Sure enough, they all had these big, clunky type-writers on their laps. They were furiously tapping away at them, their faces almost buried in the keys.

"Hey!" I hollered to them when I was close enough. "Shoeless Joe Jackson is innocent! You've got to print that!"

"What?" they asked, looking up at me.

"The Series is fixed!" I shouted. "But Joe Jackson had nothing to do with it. It's up to you to tell the world. If you don't, he'll be thrown out of baseball for the rest of his life."

Well, they must have thought that was just about the funniest thing they had ever heard in their lives. A few of them couldn't stop laughing.

"That's a good one, kid!"

"The Reds whupped the Sox fair and square," added another reporter. "Don't you worry about Shoeless Joe and the Sox. They'll come back tomor-row."

"No, they won't!" I yelled. "They're playing to lose! You've got to believe me!"

"Kid, we're on deadline," one of the reporters told me. "Why don't you go home and let us do our job?"

"Yeah, go play with your toys, sonny."

The reporters turned back to their typewriters, and the keys began click-clacking again. They didn't want to listen to me.

I had done all I could do. The fix was on. It was only a matter of time before the scandal would be exposed. Shoeless Joe, who hadn't done anything wrong, would be caught up in it and his life would be ruined.

I might as well go back home, I thought to myself. I took a seat and pulled one of my shiny new baseball cards out of my pocket. There was nothing to do but relax, let the tingling sensation wash over me, and I'd disappear. In the back of my mind, I still felt there was something I could do for Shoeless Joe. I just didn't know what it was.

That's when another idea hit me. So *what* if I couldn't prevent the Black Sox Scandal from happening? So what if I couldn't save Joe's reputation? I could do something even *better*.

I could take Joe Jackson back home *with* me.

## 20

# A Different World

BY THIS TIME, THE USHERS AND SECURITY PEOPLE HAD left the ballpark. I went down to the front row and hopped the fence onto the field. The Sox dugout was empty. The door at the back of the dugout wasn't locked. I opened it and went into the tunnel that connected the dugout to the locker room.

Fortunately, the Sox were still there. I followed the sound of their voices until I reached the locker room. Some of the players had showered and were getting dressed. Others were still sitting at their lockers in their dirty uniforms. Nobody seemed to care when I came in.

There was a lot of tension in the room. I could feel it. Kid Gleason, the manager, was stalking around, glaring at everybody. Chick Gandil was talking quietly with Eddie Cicotte. Cicotte must have said something funny, because Gandil started laughing.

When Kid Gleason saw Gandil laugh, something must have snapped in him. Even though Gandil was about six inches taller and fifty pounds heavier, Gleason suddenly leaped toward the first baseman and wrapped his hands around his throat.

"You think losing is funny, Gandil?" he shouted as he tried to strangle the bigger man. "You like to lose?"

The other players separated the two men before any punches could be thrown. But the damage was done. A few minutes later, Ray Schalk, the catcher, attacked Eddie Cicotte and had to be pulled off him.

Gloom filled the locker room. I saw Joe Jackson sitting at his locker, his head down, hands on his face. Swede Risberg came over to Joe before I could get to him.

"You looked pretty good out there today, Jackson," he said. It wasn't a compliment, I could tell.

"Thanks," Joe said softly, his head still in his hands.

"You're making the rest of us look bad," Swede continued, lowering his voice so the others wouldn't hear.

Joe looked up, anger in his eyes.

"Then play like you want to win," he said.

I thought he might take a swing at Risberg, but he didn't and Swede went off to take a shower. I pulled up the stool next to Joe.

"This ain't no place for a boy, Stosh," he said. "You oughta get out of here. Go on home."

"I need to talk to you first, Joe. This is important."

"There's nothin' Ah can do," Joe said glumly. "Ah played my best. The other guys—"

"There *is* something you can do, Joe!" I said. "You can get out of here! Get out before it's too late!"

He looked up at me. "What are you talkin' 'bout? Where am Ah gonna go?"

"Joe, you're not going to believe what I'm about to tell you. But you have to, for your own good. I live in the future, and I can take you there with me."

Joe looked at me, expressionless.

"Ah thought you said you lived in Louisville."

"I do! I live in Louisville in the twenty-first century. I traveled over eighty years back in time with a baseball card to meet you. Now I'm going to go back, and I can take you with me."

A little smile snuck into the corners of Joe's mouth. "You gotta be kiddin', Stosh."

"I'm not kidding!" I said, reaching into my pocket excitedly. "Look. You see this camera? You've never seen a camera like this, have you? That's because it doesn't exist in your time. And these baseball cards? Look at these statistics on the back. I come from the future, Joe!"

Joe took one of the cards and examined it. Then I remembered he couldn't read, so I told him the name of the player on the card was Barry Bonds, and that he'd hit seventy-three homers in the 2001 season.

"Ah ain't never heard of no ballplayer named Bonds."

"That's because he plays in the *future*, Joe! He

hasn't even been born yet."

"Seventy-three homers in a season?" Joe chuckled. "Aw, c'mon, Stosh! Nobody could do that. Nobody ever hit *thirty* homers in one year."

"Joe, he *did* it!" I insisted. "It's a whole different world in the future. I could take you with me and your life will be completely different."

Joe looked at me again, like he was trying to decide whether or not to believe me.

"They got baseball where you live?" he asked.

"Sure they do! And in the future, players like you make millions of dollars a year! You'll be a rich man. And we've got cool stuff like DVD players, the Internet, and video games."

Joe thought it over for a minute or so, a puzzled look on his face. He kept looking over at me, as if he was expecting me to say "April fool!" or something.

"Thanks, anyway, Stosh," he said, shaking his head. "But even if you could do what you say you can, Ah got Katie to think about. We wanna have kids someday. And Ah got to think about my mama, too. Ah can't go running out on them. Not at a time like this."

"Joe, all your troubles will be over if you come with me."

"Ah maybe can't read," Joe said, "but Ah know this much. A man can't solve no problem by runnin' away from it. Thanks, but Ah think Ah'll stay put right here."

There was no convincing him. He stuck out his hand, and I shook it.

"Good luck, Joe."

"You too, Stosh."

As I left the Sox locker room and made my way out of the ballpark, I was feeling pretty good. While I hadn't exactly succeeded in my mission, I had given it my best shot. I felt a sense of satisfaction for at least *trying* to do something good.

Even if Joe had agreed to come home with me, it might have been a big mistake. Where would he live in the future? How could a guy who couldn't read or write survive in the twenty-first century?

I figured I would go back to that park where I had seen Joe playing ball with those boys earlier in the day. Maybe I could find a nice, quiet, grassy spot under a tree where I could relax for a few minutes and prepare for my trip back home.

I was thinking those pleasant thoughts when two big guys jumped me from behind.

# 21

# The Right Thing

A HAND CAME OUT OF NOWHERE, COVERED MY MOUTH, and wrapped around my face. The hand smelled of cigars. I had no time to react. Another guy grabbed my arms and twisted them behind my back. It hurt, and I was scared.

"We been lookin' for you," a gruff voice spat in my ear.

They were holding my head, but out of the corners of my eyes I could see that the two guys were the same two guys I'd encountered in the basement of that billiard parlor when I first arrived in 1919: Abe and Billy. They worked for that gambler Rothstein.

"You gonna scream if I take my hand off your mouth?" Billy asked. I shook my head, and he took his hand away. They kept their grip on my hands behind my back, though.

"That was pretty sharp, kid, the way you got out of that hotel room closet."

"I was scared."

"You better be more scared *now*."

"Are you going to lock me up again?"

"No, we're gonna hurt you."

My eyes bugged out.

"Kid, I *told* you that if you ran away, I would have to hurt you. I'm a man who keeps my promises."

*I should have listened to my mother. I should have listened to my mother. I should have listened to my mother.*

I kept repeating it to myself. How stupid I was! My mother *warned* me that it would be dangerous to go back in time again. She *told* me that the more I did it, the bigger the chance that something would go wrong. But, no, I had to go and listen to what my math teacher said about probability. And now I was going to get beaten up, maybe killed.

As they marched me down the street, I looked around for a policeman or somebody. *Somebody* would have to notice these guys were taking me somewhere against my will. *Somebody* would do something about it.

But nobody seemed to notice. All the Cincinnati fans were still giddily celebrating the outcome of the game.

I couldn't fight back. They were too big for me. When I decided to just stop walking, they grabbed my shoulders and dragged me. They dragged me into the billiard parlor and carried me roughly down the steps into the basement.

Rothstein was sitting there. There was even more money on the table than last time. Rothstein was counting thick stacks of bills.

"We found him, Mr. Rothstein," Billy reported.

"Where was he?"

"We spotted him talking to some newspaper guys at the ballpark," Abe replied. "Then he went into the Sox dugout. We followed him out of the ballpark. We don't know where he was goin' next."

"Good work, boys." Rothstein ordered, "Tie him to the chair."

Abe pushed me down in the chair, while Billy grabbed some rope from a shelf. I could feel my heart beating in my chest. They wrapped the rope around me again and again until it just about covered my chest, arms, and legs. Then they pulled it tight and knotted it in several places. I tried to move my arms, but they were tight against the chair. I could feel sweat beading on my forehead and dripping under my arms.

When he was satisfied that I wasn't going anywhere, Rothstein got up and walked over to me. I looked to see if he was carrying a gun, but I didn't see one.

"Who did you talk to?" Rothstein demanded.

"Nobody."

"I think you're lying."

Of *course* I was lying. What else could I do?

"Are you going to shoot me?" I asked.

"No," Rothstein replied. "I don't shoot people."

I let out a sigh of relief.

"*Billy's* gonna shoot you."

I thought I was going to die right there. Billy pulled a revolver out of his belt and started sliding bullets into it. I gasped.

"Please!" I begged. "I'm just a kid. I didn't mean to hurt anybody. I just wanted to do the right thing."

"Sometimes the right thing is actually the wrong thing," Rothstein explained. "You did the wrong thing, kid. So now I have to do the right thing."

"I won't say a word! I swear it! Please don't kill me."

Billy had finished loading the gun. I'm no crybaby, but I couldn't help but start crying. My life was about to come to an end.

"I don't see that I have any choice but to kill you," Rothstein told me. "You ran away from me once and you went blabbing. If I let you go now, you'll probably go blabbing some more. I can't have you telling newspaper boys what we're up to. This is business, sonny boy. I got a lot of dough riding on this Series. I won't let you mess things up for me."

Rothstein stepped aside and motioned for Billy to do what he had to do. Billy stood in front of me and raised the gun.

"Wait!" I shouted. I had one last, desperate idea.

"What?" Billy asked.

"I have a last request," I said. "Aren't you supposed to give somebody one last request before you kill them?"

"Whaddaya want," Abe asked, "your teddy bear?"

"No," I said. "There's some baseball cards in my pocket. My left pants pocket. I want to hold one in my hand when I die. It means a lot to me. And I want a minute of silence before you shoot me. That's all I ask for."

Billy looked at Rothstein. Rothstein nodded. Abe reached into my pocket and pulled out one of my baseball cards. The ropes were holding my hands down, so he put the card between my fingers.

"Okay, kid," Billy said. "You happy now? You got one minute."

I closed my eyes and tried to forget about what was happening to me. I tried to think about where I wanted to go. The future. I wanted to go back to my own time. I wanted to be safe again.

"Make it snappy, kid," Abe muttered. "We ain't got all day."

Soon the tingling sensation arrived in my fingertips. I kept thinking about going back to my own time as the tingles moved up my hands, my arms, my chest. It was the most wonderful feeling in the world.

"What's happening?" Rothstein asked, alarmed.

The tingling sensation washed down my body.

"He's gettin' lighter! He's disappearin', boss!"

"That's impossible."

The tingling sensation washed down my legs.

"Shoot him! He's getting away!"

As I felt myself fading away from 1919, the ropes that had been holding me tight against the chair began to slip down where my body had been sitting.

I heard a gunshot.

The bullet slammed into the back of the chair I had been sitting in.

But I was gone.

# 22

# The Favor

I OPENED MY EYES, AFRAID THAT I MIGHT STILL BE sitting in the foul-smelling basement of that poolroom. I was afraid that I might be dead.

There was a big cardboard cutout of Ken Griffey, Jr., in front of me, and it was the sweetest sight I'd ever seen. I was lying on the floor in Flip's Fan Club. I felt my chest to see if there was a bullet hole or blood there. I was alive.

I looked around. The walls of Flip's were almost bare. I guessed that Flip had sold off just about everything in the store. There was a new sign on the door: GOING OUT OF BUSINESS.

I stood up. Flip was sitting in his chair, putting some cards into boxes.

"Stosh!" he said, surprised. "I didn't see you come in."

"I . . . just got here," I replied. "Are you still open?"

"Tomorrow morning I have to close the store for good. Then I'll watch your last game and I'll be officially retired."

I shook my head. I was still getting over what had happened to me, thankful that I was alive. Nothing else mattered.

"You okay, Stosh?" Flip asked. "You look a little pale. What's with the old-time clothes? You goin' to a costume party?"

"No." I chuckled. "Remember when you told me about Shoeless Joe Jackson?"

"Yeah."

"And I told you I could travel through time with baseball cards?"

"Yeah." Flip snickered.

"Well . . . I just got back from 1919," I said. "I actually met Shoeless Joe Jackson."

Flip laughed. I went through my pockets to make sure I had all my stuff.

"You crack me up," he said. "Oh, I'm gonna miss you kids."

"Flip, when you gave me that baseball card, I told you I was going to do you a favor someday. Remember?"

"Sure, but you don't have to do me any favors, Stosh."

"I want to."

I reached into my pocket and pulled out the two scraps of paper Joe Jackson had autographed for me.

"Here," I said, handing them to Flip. "I want you to have these."

Flip took the papers and looked at them. One of the scraps was burned at the edge from Shoeless Joe's candle.

At first, Flip didn't seem to understand what he was holding. But then, slowly, his eyes widened. He grabbed for his magnifying glass and examined the scraps of paper carefully.

Flip's jaw dropped open, and he looked at me. Now he knew. In his hand were two copies of the most valuable signature from the last two hundred years. In his hand was the equivalent of one million dollars.

"These look authentic," he whispered, his hand trembling.

"I know they are."

"Where'd you get 'em, Stosh?"

"Joe Jackson wrote them out for me personally," I replied. "Like I told you, I can travel through time."

Flip looked at me. It was the same look Shoeless Joe had on his face when I told him I could travel through time.

"They're for you, Flip," I said. "Maybe now you can buy a real baseball team, like you've always wanted."

Well, I've seen a few grown-ups cry in my life. But never like this. It was like Niagara Falls going down his face. He tried to give me back the autographs, but I wouldn't take them.

"Stosh, I don't know how you got these," Flip

said, wiping his eyes with his handkerchief, "but I thank you."

He got up, went over to the door, and ripped up the GOING OUT OF BUSINESS sign.

# 23

# An Old Friend

FLIP WAS NICE ENOUGH TO DRIVE ME HOME (AFTER ALL, I *did* give him a million bucks!). Neither of us said much in the car. I think we were both still a little blown away by what had happened. And all because of a silly little baseball card.

"Joey!" my mother shouted when she opened the front door. She hugged me like she didn't ever want to let go. "I'm so glad you're back!"

"Mrs. Stoshack, your son is a remarkable boy," Flip told my mom.

"Don't I know it!"

Mom tried to get Flip to come in for a cup of coffee, but he told her he had some errands to run. I knew his first errand would be to get those Shoeless Joe Jackson autographs into a safe.

"How was your trip, sweetie?" Mom asked as we went inside.

"It was . . . different," I admitted. No way I was going to tell my mother that somebody shot at me and I'd been probably a millisecond or two away from getting killed.

"Different?" Mom looked concerned. "What happened?"

"Nothin'. Hey, what do we have to eat, Mom? I'm starved."

As we walked into the kitchen, I was surprised to see an old man sitting in a wheelchair. He had a hearing aid in his ear.

"Who's the old guy?" I whispered to my mother, just to make sure the old guy couldn't hear me. Mom looked at me, a puzzled expression on her face. The TV was on, but the guy was asleep.

"What did you say?"

"I said who's the old guy?" I repeated. "What's up with the guy in the wheelchair?"

"Are you joking, Joey?"

"No," I replied. She was looking at me really strangely. "How am I supposed to know who he is? I never saw this guy in my life."

"Joey, that's Uncle Wilbur! He's been living with us for years! You know that, don't you?"

"I . . . thought he was dead."

"That's a terrible thing to say, Joey!"

She put her hand on my forehead, the way she does when she thinks I have a fever. "Are you okay? Where's your medicine?"

"I . . . must have left it in 1919."

The old guy in the wheelchair opened his eyes and looked at me. I looked at him. And I could see, right there, a faint resemblance. Suddenly it was all clear to me. This wrinkled old man, maybe a hundred years old, was the same Wilbur Kozinsky I had met when he was a boy in 1919!

"Hello, Joseph," he said weakly, waving at me.

"I think I need a drink of water," I said, sitting in the chair next to Wilbur Kozinsky.

As my mother went to get me a drink, I looked at the old man in wonder. Uncle Wilbur. I'd saved his life by giving him my flu medicine. I put my hand on his shoulder to prove to myself that he was real. I *had* changed history.

"Your sister, Gladys," I whispered to Uncle Wilbur. "What happened to her?"

"Gladys died many years ago, Joseph. You know that."

My mother came back with a tall glass of water and I took a long swig of it. Uncle Wilbur looked at the TV set.

"So I guess you didn't change history, eh?" Mom asked me, running her fingers through my hair.

I looked at her. Did she know what I had done?

"You weren't able to stop the Black Sox Scandal, were you?"

"Oh. No, I tried to stop it. But there was nothing I could do."

"Was it just a big waste of time?" Mom asked.

"Oh, I wouldn't say that, Mom." I looked at

Uncle Wilbur. "No, it certainly wasn't a waste of time at all."

Uncle Wilbur turned from the TV suddenly and looked at me.

"Hey, Joseph," he said.

"Yeah?"

"I want to ask you a question."

"What is it?"

"Where'd you get those pants?"

And I could be wrong, but I thought I saw him shoot me a wink.

# Life Isn't Fair

"C'MON, MILLER," I SHOUTED FROM MY POSITION AT FIRST base. "Let's get this thing over with!"

I was somewhere between angry and furious, maybe closer to furious. There we were, cruising along with a one-run lead in the bottom of the last inning. The leadoff guy for Yampell Jewelers had fouled out to our catcher, and the next guy bumped an easy grounder up the first baseline. I smothered it and stepped on the bag for the second out. One more out and we would be world champs. Well, champs of the Louisville Little League anyway. Pretty amazing, considering that half our team was away playing in some traveling soccer tournament.

When the next batter lofted a lazy fly to right-field, I was sure we had won it. I was ready to run off the field and grab the trophy they give the winning team.

But Michael Barton, our right fielder, booted the ball. I couldn't believe it! It tipped off his glove and rolled all the way to the fence. By the time Barton got to the ball and threw it in, the batter was sliding into third.

"C'mon, Barton!" I hollered. "What do you think you've got a glove for?"

"That's enough of that, Mr. Stoshack!" Mr. Kane took off his ump's mask and walked halfway to first base. "What did I tell you about unsportsmanlike behavior?"

"Okay, okay . . ."

I kicked the dirt disgustedly. We'd had the game in the bag, but now everything was different. If the runner on third scored, it would be a tie game. I hate tie games.

"Settle down, boys," Coach Tropiano shouted. "Just get this next guy out and it's all over."

The next "guy" was actually a girl—Jennifer Cossaboon. There were a few girls on my teams when I was in the minors, but by the time we got to the majors, all the girls had switched to softball except Jennifer. She could play the game. She didn't throw like a girl or anything. And she could hit better than some of the boys.

"Get a hit, Jenny!" somebody shouted from the bleachers.

"Strike her out, Miller!" shouted somebody else.

Jennifer stepped into the batter's box and looked to her third base coach for a sign. She knew how to bunt, I remembered. But I didn't think the Jewelers would try to squeeze the run home from third. If we threw him out at the plate, they'd look really stupid. I took one step back and a step toward the line to guard against an extra base hit.

"The play is to first base," hollered Coach Tropiano, clapping his hands. "Get the easy out."

Miller went into his windup, and Jennifer let the first pitch go by.

"Strike one!" called Mr. Kane.

"Nice pitch!" I hollered to Miller. "Two more like that, baby!"

Jennifer stepped out of the box for a moment. The parents on both sides of the field started shouting encouragement to everybody. I think some of them were more nervous than their kids.

As Miller went into his windup again, I got into my "baseball ready" position. Coach Tropiano tells us to always be thinking about what we will do if the ball is hit our way. I knew what I would do. I would grab it and step on the bag. Game over. We win.

But the ball wasn't hit my way. Jennifer smacked a grounder to short. Greg Horwitz moved a little to his right. He blocked it with his glove, and the ball rolled a few feet away from him.

The runner streaked down the third baseline.

Jennifer dropped the bat and sprinted for first.

I ran to the bag to get ready for Greg's throw.

Greg picked up the ball.

Mr. Kane ran up the first baseline so he could make the call.

I put my foot on the bag and stretched my glove out as far as I could reach.

Greg threw the ball, and it was on target.

I waited for the ball to get to me. If the ball hit my glove before Jennifer's foot hit the bag, she would be out and we would be the champs. But if her foot hit the bag before the ball hit my glove, she would be safe and the runner on third would score the tying run. I could tell it was going to be close. Real close. Everybody was screaming, but I was only listening for one sound.

*Pop. Pop.*

The first pop was Jennifer's foot hitting the first-base bag. The second pop was the ball hitting my glove.

Shoot! She was safe! I looked to Mr. Kane for the call.

"You're out!" he shouted.

Out? I couldn't believe it. Mr. Kane had blown a crucial call for the second week in a row! Only this time, I wasn't complaining. All the guys on Flip's Fan Club ran to the mound and mobbed Miller. We were the champions of the Louisville Little League. Everybody was going crazy.

But we weren't nearly as nuts as the Yampell Jewelers were. Their players and parents were all over Mr. Kane, screaming at him, cursing him out, threatening him, and telling him that he was blind as a bat. I couldn't blame them. But there was nothing they could do. The umpire's decision is final.

When it was all over, everybody on Flip's Fan Club gathered around Flip Valentini, and the mayor of Louisville presented us with the trophy. Everybody cheered and took pictures of us.

Flip leaned over and whispered into my ear, "She was safe, wasn't she?"

"Yeah," I said, with a little giggle.

"Life isn't fair, is it?"

"No, it's not," I replied. "But things usually even out in the end."

# Facts and Fictions

EVERYTHING YOU READ IN THIS BOOK WAS TRUE. THAT is, except for the stuff I made up. It's only fair to let you know which was which.

Joe Stoshack does not exist. He and his mother and the Kozinsky twins are fictional characters. It is not possible, as far as we know, to travel back in time—with or without a baseball card. I found the photos of "Gladys and Wilbur Kozinsky" in a box of old photos in an antique store.

The information about the influenza epidemic of 1918 is true. In recent studies, it has been estimated that as many as *one hundred million people* died from the disease in that one year. Recently, two flu medicines, Tamiflu and Relenza, were introduced. According to doctors I spoke with, if these medicines had existed in 1918, they might have saved lives.

Shoeless Joe Jackson was a real person, and I tried to describe him and his life as accurately as possible. This was easy, thanks to such excellent books as *Say It Ain't So, Joe!* by Donald Gropman and *Eight Men Out* by Eliot Asinof. I also watched the movies *Eight Men Out* and *Field of Dreams*, in which Joe Jackson is a character.

Joe Jackson had a spectacular World Series in 1919. He got twelve hits (more than any other player) to set a World Series record. His batting average was .375. He scored five runs and drove in six. He hit the only home run in the Series. He made sixteen putouts and didn't make a single error.

Despite his performance, Joe and seven of his teammates were suspended at the end of the 1920 season when it was revealed that the White Sox had intentionally lost the 1919 World Series to the Cincinnati Reds. They were indicted by a grand jury and put on trial. All eight were found not guilty, but baseball's first commissioner Kenesaw Mountain Landis banned them from professional baseball anyway. It was his first official act as commissioner. The "eight men out" were not allowed to play, coach, manage, or have anything to do with professional baseball for the rest of their lives.

The gamblers who arranged the World Series fix were never punished or even put on trial. However, gambling *did* catch up with Arnold Rothstein, who had put up $80,000 for the fix and won $270,000. In

1928 he lost $320,000 in a poker game. Rothstein refused to pay the money, so his opponent shot and killed him. The photo of Rothstein also came from an antique store.

The most famous story of the Black Sox Scandal tells of Joe Jackson leaving the courthouse after being indicted. A little boy came up to him and said pleadingly, "Say it ain't so, Joe."

The story is a myth. It never happened.

It's also a myth that Joe Jackson lived out the remainder of his life disgraced, pathetic, and penniless. Even though he never learned how to read or write, Joe and his wife, Katie, ran a dry cleaning business, a restaurant, a poolroom, a farm, and a liquor store in his hometown of Greenville, South Carolina. Joe was illiterate, but he was not stupid. He made a better living as a businessman than he ever did as a ballplayer.

But baseball was his true love. After he was banned from the game, Joe didn't stop playing. In the summers, he was frequently spotted on semipro teams, sometimes using a fake name. He was always discovered, though—because he was so much better than the other players.

Joe Jackson died of a heart attack on December 5, 1951, at the age of sixty-three. He is buried in Woodlawn Memorial Park in Greenville. Eight years later Katie passed away. They had no children. I was unable to track down a photo of Katie Jackson from the 1919 era. The photo of her is another antique store find.

Over the years there have been many efforts to clear the name of Joe Jackson so he can be inducted into the National Baseball Hall of Fame. Major League Baseball has stubbornly refused to consider his case.

But these are the facts about Shoeless Joe Jackson:

• He was never in communication with any gamblers.

• He never attended any of the meetings his teammates held to discuss throwing the World Series.

• He turned down big money offers to throw games—twice.

• A teammate threw an envelope containing $5,000 on his bed.

• He tried to give the money to White Sox owner, Charles Comiskey, and tell him the Series was fixed.

• Comiskey refused to see him, and Joe was instructed to keep the money.

• When all else failed, he asked to be benched before Game 1.

• His request was denied, and he went on to have the best Series of any player on either team.

In a glass display case in the Baseball Hall of Fame is a pair of Shoeless Joe Jackson's baseball shoes. Joe deserves more than that. He deserves a plaque in the Hall of Fame, too. Baseball made a big mistake in 1921, banning one of its greatest and most popular players.

If you would like Joe Jackson reinstated and inducted into the Hall of Fame, go to Shoeless Joe Jackson's Virtual Hall of Fame (www.blackbetsy.com) or write to The Shoeless Joe Jackson Society at: 106 Century Oaks Drive, Easley, SC 29642.

# Shoeless Joe Jackson's Career Statistics

| | Year | Games | At Bats | Runs | Hits | Doubles | Triples | Home Runs | Runs Batted In | Stolen Bases | Batting Average | Slugging Average |
|---|---|---|---|---|---|---|---|---|---|---|---|---|
| **Philadelphia** | 1908 | 5 | 23 | 0 | 3 | 0 | 0 | 0 | 3 | 0 | .130 | .130 |
| | 1909 | 5 | 14 | 3 | 5 | 0 | 0 | 0 | 3 | 0 | .294 | .294 |
| **Cleveland** | 1910 | 20 | 75 | 15 | 29 | 2 | 5 | 1 | 11 | 4 | .387 | .587 |
| | 1911 | 147 | 571 | 126 | 233 | 45 | 19 | 7 | 83 | 41 | .408 | .590 |
| | 1912 | 152 | 572 | 121 | 226 | 44 | 26 | 3 | 90 | 35 | .395 | .579 |
| | 1913 | 148 | 528 | 109 | 197 | 39 | 17 | 7 | 71 | 26 | .373 | .551 |
| | 1914 | 122 | 453 | 61 | 153 | 22 | 13 | 3 | 53 | 22 | .338 | .464 |
| **Cleveland/ Chicago***  } | 1915 | 128 | 461 | 63 | 142 | 20 | 14 | 5 | 81 | 16 | .308 | .445 |
| | 1916 | 155 | 592 | 91 | 202 | 40 | 21 | 3 | 78 | 24 | .341 | .495 |
| | 1917 | 146 | 538 | 91 | 162 | 20 | 17 | 5 | 75 | 13 | .301 | .429 |
| | 1918 | 17 | 65 | 9 | 23 | 2 | 2 | 1 | 20 | 3 | .354 | .492 |
| | 1919 | 139 | 516 | 79 | 181 | 31 | 14 | 7 | 96 | 9 | .351 | .506 |
| | 1920 | 146 | 570 | 105 | 218 | 42 | 20 | 12 | 121 | 9 | .382 | .589 |
| **Total** | | 1,330 | 4,981 | 873 | 1,774 | 307 | 168 | 54 | 785 | 202 | .356 | .518 |

# World Series Statistics

| Year | Games | At Bats | Runs | Hits | Doubles | Triples | Home Runs | Runs Batted In | Stolen Bases | Batting Average | Slugging Average |
|---|---|---|---|---|---|---|---|---|---|---|---|
| 1917 | 6 | 23 | 4 | 7 | 0 | 0 | 0 | 2 | 1 | .304 | .304 |
| 1919 | 8 | 32 | 5 | 12 | 3 | 0 | 1 | 6 | 0 | .375 | .563 |

*Joe Jackson was traded to the Chicago White Sox in August.

# Permissions

The author would like to acknowledge the following for use of photographs and artwork:

Nina Wallace: $x$, 126; Cincinnati Museum Center, Cincinnati, O.H.: 54; George Brace: 105, 115, 117; National Baseball Hall of Fame Library, Cooperstown, N.Y.: 107, 108, 110, 118.

**DAN GUTMAN** is the author of many books for young readers, including four other Baseball Card Adventures: HONUS & ME, JACKIE & ME, BABE & ME, and MICKEY & ME. When he is not writing books, Dan is very often visiting a school. He lives in Haddonfield, New Jersey, with his wife, Nina, and their children, Sam and Emma.

You can visit him at his website **www.dangutman.com**